# THE CIRCLE OF ALWAYS BECOMING

## JAMES ARGOS

The Circle of Always Becoming, Pathless Forest Series, Volume 1
ISBN: 978-0-578-78014-6

Cover and book production by All Things Book,
allthingsbook.org.

Library of Congress Cataloging-in-Publication Data
is available upon request.

# THE
# CIRCLE OF
# ALWAYS
# BECOMING

# CHAPTER ONE

Trapped with nothing more than the clothes he is wearing, Tobias Whitefield sprawls, face down, across a pink granite boulder, rising three feet above the whitewater tumble, swirl, and crash of the Red River roaring through its narrow canyon. *How,* he thinks, *could anyone be so stupid, so unaware as to let this happen?* As his heartbeat slows to normal, Tobias takes a deep, calming breath, pushes himself onto his hands and knees, then draws himself into a sitting position.

Upstream, the river runs against a weathered pink granite cliff.

Downstream, back the way he had come, Tobias watches the last of the flotilla of interlocked branches, onto which leaves and small gravel had accumulated, and he had mistaken for solid ground, come unattached from the cliff and disappear into the river.

Through the canyon's quarter-mile wide entrance, Tobias notices both moons closely trailing the rising sun.

Tilting his head back as far as possible, Tobias can't see the clifftop, but judging from the opposite canyon wall, he guesses it to be more than a thousand feet high.

Thinking aloud, Tobias whispers. "Two options. I can jump into the river and hope to swim the hundred feet to what I hope is solid ground before the river dashes me against a rock or into the cliff, or pulls me under and drowns me. Or, I can leap to the cliff and hope I can climb a thousand vertical feet without falling. Is that even possible?"

Tobias bites his upper lip, the pain inspiring a third option. "What if, instead of climbing up, I climb sideways along the cliff?" A single glance convinces Tobias of such a plan's futility. Twenty feet downstream from the boulder he sits upon, the cliff changes from pink granite with plenty of possible hand and footholds to greasy, black schist with none.

Not attempting the impossible task of outshouting the river's roar, Tobias asks, "Old Friend," his name for God, "Why are you doing this? Why have you stripped me of my mate and child? Why did You drive me into exile? Why must I die?

"I know entering the Forbidden Mountains is wrong and inexcusable, but if You hadn't taken my wife or forced me to leave Salem, I wouldn't be here. If You look into my heart, you won't find what the High Priest believes I've become—an evil man, because I am without a wife or child—but you'll find a grief-racked soul who loves You and always will.

"You saw, if You were watching, a man who allowed himself for a few precious moments to become distracted by a dozen crows picking something gold and shiny out of the gravel. You're right; when I realized I had, without knowing, crossed the line and entered the Red River's Canyon, and in doing so entered the Forbidden Mountains, I should have immediately splayed myself upon the gravel and begged Your forgiveness, but You know better than anyone that's not my nature. You know that when I don't understand something, it's like an itch that drives me crazy until I scratch it away.

"Besides, if I had stopped and trespassed by only a few feet instead of nearly a mile, would my crime have been any less real, my punishment any less severe?

"Still, I cannot believe that the God whose first words He spoke to the Four Hundred on the Final Day of Creation were 'Fear not! For I am a God of love!' cannot find it in His heart to forgive me."

Tobias looks down at his massive hands folded in his lap, then at the boulder on which he sits. "Yet, it's also true that You placed this boulder in this precise spot to serve as my refuge. But a refuge for what purpose?"

Tobias stares into the river's whitewater foam until he can't be sure who moves—the river, or himself.

"After all, I've lost my mate, my daughter, my community; maybe I should stop struggling and welcome death. If I knew what it would take to be welcomed back into Salem, I'd have a goal to work towards. As it is, the only thing I'm sure of is that all it takes for me to reunite with my mate and daughter and live forever within God's presence is my death. Unless, as God has written in the *Holy Book of Life*, 'whosoever breaks my commandments and dies without forgiveness shall be cast into outer darkness and there remain until My heart softens and I forgive his trespass or his soul dies of loneliness.'"

Tobias looks between the cliff face and river.

"Is what I've done so bad that God, who can read my heart like an open book, cannot forgive me?"

Turning his back to the cliff, Tobias steps to the edge of the boulder. Rocking back and forward on his heels, he takes three deep breaths, tightening every muscle in anticipation of jumping. Instead, Tobias whirls, runs, and leaps, turning his head at the last moment so he hits the cliff face with only his right cheek. His arms and legs spread wide, frantically flailing until they come to rest upon irregularities in the cliff's face strong enough to hold his weight.

As he hangs, gasping for breath, Tobias thinks, *A thousand feet straight up, and if I fall, a few moments of terror and I'll stand before God and learn my fate.* Or, Tobias bites his upper lip hard enough to bleed, *I wonder how far upstream I'd have to go to find solid land?*

As soon as he has thought it, Tobias starts inching his way upstream.

• • •

Tobias, his left hand nearly at the level of his foot, his right hand and leg as high as they can reach, stares at a section of cliff that juts straight outward for a dozen feet, the side facing him sheared smooth as if cut with a knife.

"Old Friend, look! My hands are bloodied, my fingernails worn to the quick, every muscle is cramping. I'm cold, hungry, and exhausted. I can't go forward. It's useless to go back. Impossible to climb out. And now it's getting dark. Old Friend, why have you done this? Why have you made me suffer so, only to fail? Am I the punchline to some cruel joke?"

Tobias closes his eyes. How simple it would be to just lean back and let go. A few moments of terror and then—a smile flickers across his face.

For three days, after leaving Salem, Micah Skylark, the High Priest, pursued Tobias across the Great Valley. Tobias escaped by crossing the Red River and entering an area of pink granite hillocks he named the Tangled Hills. From there, he traveled north, eventually arriving at a broad, shallow valley dominated by a hundred and fifty foot red sandstone tower. A warm spring emerging from its base flowed into a pool surrounded by towering aspens.

While laying in the pool's warm water, Tobias dreamt he was standing at the Red River Canyon's entrance. Then, he was inside the canyon, as if he moved without moving as the ground passed beneath his feet. Suddenly the ground gave way, and he fell into the river. He swam not across, but down to the bottom of the river and out the other side. When he emerged, the sun was rising from behind a mountain.

It was this dream that inspired Tobias to seek the Red River Canyon. But the rest of the dream made little sense. The ground falling out from beneath his feet could be the death of his mate and daughter. The moving without moving might mean something would happen without his say in the matter. But, until this very moment, he hadn't an inkling what it might mean to swim down through a river and out the other side.

But now, after two days of hanging inches above certain death, Tobias takes a deep breath and thinks, *Why not?* He takes a second, slower, deeper breath. *At least I'll die trying.* A third, even slower and deeper breath. *In the dream, I don't die.* After a fourth deep breath, Tobias pushes off the cliff and plunges into the river.

The cliff jutting into the river has created a pocket of calmer water. Tobias swims down and forward. Just as he is about to encounter the full blast of the river's current, he discovers the cliff is undercut. He reaches out and grasps a ledge as his legs pivot above his head. His legs, outstretched halfway, hit solid rock. Upside down, he hobbles against the current. Then, as his lungs feel they are about to burst, his feet straighten. With a push born of desperation, Tobias spins and bobs into a pocket of air.

After pulling himself into a cavity formed by a large section of the cliff falling and shattering, Tobias, pinching his shoulders together, slithers through a crack and onto a jagged boulder. From there, it's but a short leap onto dry, solid ground.

"Old Friend, thank you. I'm safe."

Exhausted and desperate for sleep, Tobias stretches out between small angular boulders against the cliff, as far from the river as possible. Each time he closes his eyes, the river's roar and images of the dozens of times he slipped and nearly fell flood his mind. And yet, he must have slept, because he wakes long after sunrise, flailing his arms and legs like a turtle on its back.

After struggling into a sitting position, Tobias leans

against the cliff wall. "Old Friend, two days without food, my strength is failing, and now I see the place I landed last night is nothing more than a sandbar two dozen feet on a side."

Tobias rubs the back of his neck; it's wet. Not wanting to spend the energy to stand, Tobias crawls to the far edge of the sandbar and sits upon his knees. The water streams out from between the boulders of a usually dry cascade before disappearing directly into the sand.

The cascade is choked with angular head-sized boulders and cut back into the cliff far enough that although it is steep, it's not vertical.

Tobias rubs a big hand across his face, like he is trying to rub off its features. Then, forcing himself into a standing position, he walks to the cliff, where he cups his hands and lets them fill with water.

The first time he drinks, "Old Friend, thank you." The second drink, "Rebecca, Naomi, I yearn for the day we're together." The third time, he lets the water overflow his cupped hands. "As I climb out of this canyon, may I climb back into life and one day find a way to be welcomed back to Salem." He empties his cupped hands over his head.

After a brief pause, Tobias wipes his hands dry on his ripped and filthy linen pants. Then, reaching his left hand as high as he can, he feels with his right foot for a place to rest it.

As the sun reaches its zenith, Tobias stops within sight of the clifftop. Until then, the climb had been like walking upstairs, if stairs sometimes slip out from beneath his feet, and he had to scramble to keep from sliding down. But now, the last fifty feet is a sheer cliff made slick by moss and water. After studying the cliff for five, ten, fifteen minutes, and finding no way shorter or less dangerous than another, Tobias flattens himself against the cliff and—trusting to friction, the confidence that comes hanging two days to the side of a cliff, and the belief he's meant to live—inches his way to the top.

. . .

Too hungry to stop and admire the view, Tobias follows a contour through a dense pine forest with a mat of needles too thick to allow anything more than a few hardy kinds of grass to grow. After a half hour, he hears wind moving through trees, except there's no wind. Instinctively, he moves towards the sound's source and discovers a thirty-foot waterfall on top of which sit six crows.

Staring at the waterfall, Tobias laughs to himself. In the three weeks since fleeing Salem and escaping the pursuit of the High Priest, Tobias, in an effort to make this strange and inhospitable land his home, had begun naming every river and prominent natural feature.

*Crows have been with me every step of my journey from Salem, and, despite their luring me into breaking God's commandment by entering the Forbidden Mountains, they are the closest thing I have to a friend.*

As Tobias watches, three crows fly off. He says, "To honor my friends the crows, I name this waterfall..." He winks at the three remaining crows, "...Three Crows Falls."

Hurrying toward the small pool at the base of the

waterfall, Tobias grabs handfuls of berries from shrubs growing along its shore, but slows as he finds, among river cobbles, something more important than a few berries. He finds a scattering of obsidian cobbles.

It is the work of a few moments to fashion a spearpoint and find a reasonably straight branch into which he can jam it.

An hour later, Tobias has speared a fish, made a fire ring of double-fist-sized cobbles, and sparked a fire with the obsidian cobbles.

After sating his hunger, Tobias climbs atop one of two dozen boulders scattered into a natural labyrinth. Lying back, the sun warming and relaxing his body, Tobias plummets in and out of sleep until startling awake.

It's dark. Branches breaking. Something big moving, then falling. A growl followed by a high-pitched, almost human cry.

Tobias slides off the boulder. He runs forward into another boulder. His heart racing, his mind fueled by confusion, Tobias blindly runs into one, then another, and another boulder. Turning left, right, racing straight ahead or back, the boulders close in, until Tobias stumbles and falls. Pushing himself onto his hands and knees, then into a seated position, he shrieks, crossing his hands in front of his face as he frantically scoots back as a vague, gray curving shape looms over him.

A cloud moves from in front of Luna, the larger of the two moons, and by its light, Tobias understands he's safe. The vague shape looming over him is not a bear or mountain lion, but six feet of a still-standing dead pine.

He thinks, *Fire.*

Crawling between boulders, Tobias scoops against the pine tree's base every needle, broken branch, piece of dry moss, anything that might burn, then stops, holds his breath, and listens. Whatever happened is still happening.

Sparking a fire with two obsidian cobbles, Tobias lights the kindling. Soon, the fire blazes along the entire tree like a giant candle, blocking any stars' appearance with its smoke and light.

When Tobias wakes, the tree is a smoldering ash pile, and the sun has risen mid-morning high. He quickly finds his way out of the labyrinth.

"Old Friend, last night I dreamed I was the tree that I set ablaze. And as I burned, I became black smoke, and the smoke congealed into a black stone that rolled to the top of the Forbidden Mountains, and there it became white.

"I don't understand how or what it means for smoke to become rock. But for a rock to roll uphill is impossible without the help of some secret, unseen power. Is that what this dream means? With your help, I can surmount an impossible obstacle? My return to Salem? The black rock turning white reminds me of the Final Day of Creation, when you spoke to the Four Hundred out of a flame of ever-changing color that gave off no heat, and Your presence rested upon a large black stone. Then, when Your presence ascended and vanished in a brilliant flash of light, the black stone became white. If, in the dream, I am the black stone that becomes white, does that mean Your presence will soon leave me? Or does it mean that Your presence is resting upon me and has the power to transform me?

"To understand the dream, must I go to the summit of the Forbidden Mountains? Or is that taking the dream too literally? That I survived the Canyon Ordeal, I take as a sign that I have found Your forgiveness. And now, I have no greater desire than to follow whatever path you would have me take, whether back to Salem or to the top of the Forbidden Mountains, where, according to my dream, I might encounter Your presence. However, with nothing more than a couple of obsidian cobbles and a makeshift spear, wherever You have me go, whatever You have me do, the journey will be difficult."

Tobias starts towards Three Crows Falls, where he hopes to spear a fish for breakfast, but stops after only a few steps and drops to his knees. He retouches the edge of the spearpoint to a sharp knife-edge and slices a large chunk off the rump of a freshly killed deer, the source of the frightening sounds that last night drove Tobias to the center of the labyrinth.

After cooking the meat in the fire pit he used to prepare the fish, Tobias eats until his stomach bulges.

Early afternoon, his feast finished, Tobias climbs to the top of a boulder in the Circle of Stones. *Downhill, I return to living alone, with no purpose other than surviving. Uphill, where a dream tells me to go, I might meet and be transformed by God. Is it possible that by breaking God's commandment, I was obeying God's will? Is it possible I'm where God wants me to be, doing what God wants me to do? If that's the case, I have no choice but to take the path leading into the Forbidden Mountains' heart.*

. . .

Two days later, Tobias camps between the walls of a large boulder surrounded by willows and wind-sheared junipers that split in two and worked itself apart enough to form a narrow slot that he can heat with a small fire, its sides radiating heat long after the flame has gone out.

In the morning, a marmot, warming its sluggish body, becomes Tobias's breakfast. After breakfast and the sun have warmed the thin air, Tobias leaves his sheltered camp's warmth and comfort and turns into a cold breeze flowing off the highest peaks.

"Old Friend, the closer I come to the mountaintop, the more uncertain I become. It's one thing to return into Your presence after death, but encountering Your presence while I live terrifies me."

The first three miles gently climb through treeless, lush meadows. The final approach is nearly as steep as the rock-choked cascade he climbed out of the Red River Canyon and is covered with thin granite plate-lets that continually slide from beneath his feet in a near-constant avalanche unless he walks in long, sweep-ing arcs. Just as he approaches the saddle between the two highest peaks, the wind blasts him back and nearly off his feet. The higher he climbs, the stronger the wind, until finally he drops to his hands and knees and crawls the final few feet to the cliff edge. Through narrow slits, Tobias looks down into a nearly perfect bowl filled with dozens of ponds and rivulets a thousand feet below and across a deep narrow valley to a range of slightly lower mountains. Bubbling above the distant mountains is a line of white clouds.

Tobias winces at a silver-colored flash, then another and another. The flashing lights, caused by sunlight striking something too small to see, are confined to a narrow band, stretching from a pushed-up mound of dirt on the south side of the bowl to the top of the peak on the saddle's north side, where a chunk of the mountain is missing.

Tobias shivers, rubs his bare arms, and closes his eyes.

*If I am supposed to meet God here, where is He? If He's here, why can't I see Him? Whatever I do, I must do it quickly before the clouds arrive.* Tobias sighs. *If I go back, nothing's changed, nothing's happened.*

After eyeing possible paths down the west-facing slope, Tobias backs away from the cliff edge and, keeping low to the ground, hurries south to a narrow ridge leading off the side of the slightly lower peak. The west side is less steep and rocky, making his descent quicker and easier. When at last he arrives just above the pushed-up mound of dirt, he sprints off the ridge and, using the force of his built-up momentum, races onto its top.

Looking at the fast-approaching clouds, Tobias guesses he has less than a half hour before he needs to find shelter and make himself as small a target for lightning as possible.

Racing off the mound, Tobias hurries to its northern edge, where he discovers the silver glints of light are reflecting off something smooth and uniform in thickness and curve. Something that rock might look like if it was made in a kiln. He claws at the dirt piled against the north end and discovers that whatever it is is hollow. The strange substance, he names man-rock.

The lightning flash and thunder roar occupy a single heartbeat.

# CHAPTER TWO

After several failed attempts, Tobias manages to stand. As he brushes soft ice pellets out of his hair and off his clothes, an icy blast of wind, carrying the distant rumble of an approaching storm and an opening salvo of giant raindrops, sends him stumbling forward. He lands on the pushed-up mound, peers through the hole he had created before the near lightning strike, then frantically claws at the dirt until he's enlarged the hole enough that he's able to wiggle through and tumble onto a hard, silver-colored floor.

Lying still, Tobias listens to the howling wind pass harmlessly over him. Then, slowly, as if coming from far away, a thought grows until it can't be ignored. *It's getting lighter and warmer.*

"Old Friend, what happened? Why did you once again almost kill me, only to save me?"

While waiting for an answer, Tobias relaxes into sleep.

• • •

When he wakes hours later, Tobias is warm, dry, and bathed in soft bluish light. Grunting and groaning with effort, he manages to stand, then holds his head between his hands to keep it from splitting apart and the ground from rising, falling, and spinning around.

*This place is beyond anything any man can build. And if God made it, why is it broken?*

Every twenty feet, on both sides of the narrow hallway, there's a door without a handle or obvious way to open it. At chest height beside each door is an impression of a hand, slightly smaller than his, and beside the handprint is written LQ followed by a number, beginning with eight and growing smaller.

The doorway opposite, LQ-1, doesn't have a hand imprint, but at his approach the door hisses open and soft, slow music fills the air. The room is as big as his kitchen and the main room of his house in Salem. A tumble of eight chairs surrounds two upright tables.

At the far end of the room, a door is slightly ajar. Tobias has to push hard to get it to swing open, and as it does, it sweeps an area of floor clear of containers of every size, shape, and color. Tobias picks up a pouch the size of his hand and tears where it says to tear, then squeezes out something pink and chunky. He sniffs, tastes, thinks it too sweet, and drops the package, but quickly picks it up.

It isn't the applesauce that excites him, but the word—applesauce—written across the front of the pouch. *How*, he thinks, *is it possible that the same letters and words used by God when He wrote the Holy Book of Life are printed on the pouch?*

Tobias scrapes a section of the floor clear with his feet, then sits among the containers and reads their content. Most words he understands, but some words, like

Chinese, French, Tauren, or Cygnian, refer to types of foods he doesn't know. Some he can eat right out of the package, while others have instructions explaining how they are to be "reconstituted," a word he doesn't know the meaning of.

"Old Friend, this place was home to eight people not created upon the Final Day of Creation. How can this be? And where are they?"

Tobias opens a pouch labeled tuna and squeezes its contents onto brown rice crackers.

If there's food, there must be water.

Near the end of a long counter, Tobias finds two tubes extending over a sink. As Tobias looks for a cup and a way to turn on the water, one hand passes under a tube and cold water spills out. Cupping his hands, Tobias lets them fill with water and drinks several handfuls. At the end of the counter, directly facing him, is a tall cabinet with a painted red plus sign. Opening the cabinet, he finds bottles of all sizes and shapes. The tallest bottle contains white pills promising headache relief.

Miriam, the healer in Salem, has a powder prepared from ash tree bark, which does the same, but Tobias has seen none such tree for days. Desperate for relief, Tobias reasons that people who use the same language must know the same God, and their medicine must not be dangerous. The directions say to take one or two but no more than six in one day. After shaking out two tablets, he stares at them, licks his lips, and throws them into his mouth. Gagging and choking, Tobias rushes to the water and gulps several handfuls. After a few minutes, the foul taste and headache have vanished.

Leaving the cafeteria, Tobias continues to the doorway at the hallway's end. At his approach, the door parts in the middle and disappears into the wall on either side. In the center of the room, two chairs face away from the door. Along either side of the room are three chairs. In front of the chairs, and sunk into a wide, angled upward panel, are several rows of letters, numbers, and many strange symbols. The letters aren't arranged in any order that he can tell.

Tobias pats the back of his head in an effort to jog his mind into action. Then, standing behind the chairs in the room's center, he grasps their tops but immediately jerks his left hand back. Stepping quickly around the chair, Tobias stumbles back as if he's been hit until he's pressed against the far wall, then slides to the floor.

*I've seen dead people. I saw Rebecca and Naomi before Miriam wrapped them in shrouds, but this is much worse.*

Staring back at Tobias is a man wearing a dark blue tunic, hanging loose about leathery skin that has shriveled taut to reveal every bone in stark relief. The man's eyes are gone. His mouth is drawn into a hideous, frozen smile.

"Old Friend, I know it used to be a man. But what happened? Why does he look like that? And what is that he wears about his neck?"

Tobias crawls forward. Part of him says, *forget it*, but another part says, *you know if you don't look, you won't sleep.* Leaning forward as far as he dares, he finds a place where the thin thread of silver man-rock joined in tiny loops hangs away from the skin, then gently lays it in his hand. At the bottom of the necklace, hanging at heart level, is a small letter t.

On the floor, close to the mummified right leg, are two small objects.

One is oblong, two inches long, and three quarters of an inch thick. Along both sides are flecks of red paint, and in between are six thin slats, which have a place to hook a fingernail. He tries to pry one out but can't.

The other object is yellowish-red, flat, circular, and an inch in diameter. Embossed on one side is a picture of something moving between stars. Written around the edge is Star Voyager XXIII, and at the base the numbers 3244. The other side is embossed with the letter E entwined with a U and written around the edge, "Earth United for the Good of All."

Tobias turns the flat circular object over and over until a stabbing pain in his head, accompanied by a bright flash of light, renders him unconscious.

• • •

"Where the fuck am I? What the fuck just happened?" Staring down at the dirty rags he's wearing, he growls. "What the fuck?" Bursting through the doors leading out of the command center, he runs down the long hallway, bulls his way through the opening, and slides down the other side. Jumping to his feet, he leans back and bellows, "This ain't no goddamn star voyager but a fucking cargo ship and I ain't Tobias what-the-fuck but Erik Thorson from goddamn Idaho. And this ain't Earth because Earth don't have two goddamn moons. Where the fuck is everyone?"

By moonlight, Erik stumbles through puddles and over embedded cobbles to the largest intact cargo ship section. Squeezing through a rip in the metal, Erik waits for the lighting and heating to detect his presence. On either side of a narrow passageway are rows of people-sized tubes stacked four high. He looks inside more than a dozen biostasis chambers before deciding all four hundred are empty.

*If everybody made it out, that means the ship crashed after unloading its cargo—us. So why the fuck am I the only one here?*

Once past the biostasis units, Erik enters a large storage area. One corner is filled with all manners of clothes, including coats, gloves, and boots. But the central part contains everything—including solar generators, quantum computational interfacing units, energy shield domes, and plasma drives—that a thirty-third-century first-generation colonist would need. He grins as his eyes come to rest upon a high-security container labeled "Property of Lionel Rutger."

It takes Erik a half hour to find a low-frequency magnetic field generator—useful to keep native wildlife at bay, and, if modified in ways not strictly legal, able to disrupt any encrypted lock.

Ten minutes later, the container top unlocks with a decisive click. Erik flips open the top, then yells, "Fuck, yes! Just what the doctor ordered!" As soon as he says it, he regrets saying it. Jenny was to be the colony's doctor. "Where the fuck is Jenny? Where the fuck is everyone?"

Eric grabs a bottle labeled "Glen Eyrie Premium Scotch Whiskey" and smashes the bottle's neck against the pallet's side. *If it's good enough for Lionel Rutger, one of the richest men in the twelve star systems, it's good enough for me.* Holding the jagged edge away from his mouth, Erik pours a big swig into his throat, then tosses the bottle as far as he can and watches it shatter.

Picking up another bottle, Erik takes the time to open it properly.

Not having touched a drop of alcohol in over six years, it doesn't take Erik long to drink himself into a stupor.

Hours later, Erik wakes in a pool of vomit. His first thought is to exchange the rags he's wearing for something clean and functional, and settles on a single-piece red jumpsuit because of its abundance of pockets and a coat, gloves, and hat that can withstand sub-zero temperatures.

Returning to the cargo ship's forward section, Erik heads straight for the cafeteria's medicine cabinet, where he grabs a bottle promising headache and hangover relief. Opening the cabinet beneath the water tap, Erik grabs a large cup. Tossing the pills to the back of his throat, he chases them down with water.

Returning to the ship's bridge, Erik sits in the chair beside the mummified pilot. "I've been trying to remember. I think your name is Andrew-something, and a couple of days before leaving Earth, we got properly pissed. You've got a wife and child somewhere in the Cygnus

Quadrant, and this was your last assignment before joining them. So, why the hell did you ride the ship down?

"From the little I remember, you seemed an alright guy, and you deserve better than sitting forever at the controls of this shitpile. You deserve a proper burial. I suppose I could dig you a proper grave, and even put up a marker, but why? You bury someone so people have a place to come and remember, but if I bury you, who'll know? Who'll ever find it?"

Erik returns to the kitchen, where he shifts through packages on the floor and finds one with the slogan, "Home Planet Bistro, Genuine Earth Cuisine." The box claims to contain a complete steak, mashed potato, corn on the cob, and apple pie dinner. He shakes the box and listens to the dry contents rattle. As he puts the unopened box into the reconstitution oven, he shudders. He never wanted to know how food was reconstituted and always avoided doing it or eating it whenever possible, but now he doesn't have a choice.

While waiting for the oven to beep, Erik wades through the mess on the floor and unlatches an insulated steel door and removes two brown bottles. After touching a bottle against his cheek, he sets them inside a metal box and pushes a blue button. After a whoosh and a swirling gray cloud, Erik removes two perfectly chilled bottles of dark ale.

Five minutes later, the oven beeps. Erik opens the box and there is everything as advertised, on a ceramic plate that hadn't existed before being reconstituted. The food is as he remembers, hot and filling but bland.

After supper, Erik crosses the hallway to LQ-1, the ship captain's living quarters, which he enters by placing his hand inside the hand imprint. The door hisses open.

On the bedside table is a holographic projector. After touching the base, which immediately glows blue, Erik watches as Andrew, his wife, and daughter silently play on a swing set, then walk alongside a pond feeding geese. After a few minutes of watching, Erik slams his fist on the bed and turns the projector off. It's only then Erik realizes he's been crying. *Where the fuck is Jenny?*

Using a remote, Erik turns on ocean sounds. Instantly, the wall opposite the bed's head turns into waves lapping up on a beach with the occasional seagull flying across a deep blue, computer-generated sky. Lying back onto the bed, Erik thinks, *Six years. Seven years? And his name is Tobias? What the hell is happening? How do I know any of that?*

Erik lets images bubble up. Now, he's standing beside a beautiful woman he doesn't recognize. But he and the woman appear happy and in love.

Searching through the crowd encircling a large black rock, Erik finds Jenny standing beside another man. *Except her name isn't Jenny, it's Miriam. How do I know that?*

Hovering above the rock is a column of fire that's continually changing color. And a voice—*God's voice?* When the voice stops, the fire vanishes into a bright point of light. The black rock has turned white, and lying on top of the rock is a book.

Erik's voice in his mind asks, "Tobias, what's happening?"

"God just created the Four Hundred and gave us the *Holy Book of Life*, and now we're going to Salem, where we'll live. I'll work as a quarryman and mason, and Rebecca shall work as a potter and weaver."

"Where's Jenny?"

Tobias remains silent.

"Me and you, we're not in Salem but on a mountain top. Why?"

The scene changes, and Tobias is now driving a wagon filled with quarried stone, pulled by six horses. He is approaching a giant tree on top of a broad hill. Another man, riding a horse, approaches at full gallop.

Tobias jumps from the wagon as the man slides off the still-moving horse.

"Rebecca in labor. Miriam worried. Bad."

A second later, Tobias is on horseback, galloping past the place Erik recognizes as where Tobias claims he was created, then down off the hill to the center of town, where he turns left, goes two blocks, and jumps off. He thrusts the horse's reins into the nearest person's hands and bulls his way through the crowd pressed in close about a two-story adobe building's front door. As he turns to go up the steps, a large man blocks his path. The man says, "No. Trust me. You don't want to go in."

A high, piercing scream. Tobias flicks the man off the steps and into the crowd, then hurries down a narrow hallway and flings the door open so hard it dents the wall.

Blood. Blood everywhere. On the floor, the walls, the sheets, and the black obsidian knife that Jenny/Miriam uses to slice open Rebecca's abdomen. *A stone knife? Why?*

Tobias drops to the floor, splashing blood. A moment later, a woman helps Tobias to a chair as Jenny cuts the umbilical cord, then covers the face of the silent, still body. Jenny hands the newborn girl to Tobias.

"Naomi. Her name is Naomi."

Erik, thinking that something good has come out of this horror, asks, "How many children do you have?"

"None. Rebecca had two early-term miscarriages. This child she carried well into the eighth month."

Jenny rips the baby from Tobias's arms, and the other woman blocks his view. A few minutes later, Jenny says, "I'm sorry. The baby's heart stopped. She stopped breathing. I did everything, but it wasn't enough."

Erik thinks, *Poor bastard*, then shudders and sits up like he's waking up from a nightmare. If he's remembering Tobias's memories, and in some way he and Tobias are the same person, just as Miriam and Jenny are somehow the same person, then holy crap, what a fucking life he's had/is having.

Erik returns to the kitchen and grabs the edge of the table. The holographic projector hums, and a column of purple light shoots out of the center of the table. Speaking slow and loud, Erik commands, "Movies, comedy."

After a three-movie marathon, accompanied by six bottles of beer, Erik returns to the captain's living quarters and drops into a deep sleep.

• • •

Erik wakes and asks, "What's the time?"

A voice floating on the air states, "The time is 11:43 p.m., Feb 16, 3254 GMT."

"No, what time is it here?"

"Earth equivalent time is 5:15 a.m., July 1."

"What's the weather?"

"Temperature −8 degrees Centigrade, wind westerly 20 kph, sky clear."

Erik swings himself out of bed, then staggers into the bathroom and stares at himself in the mirror. "Let's see. I left Earth in 3245, which makes me thirty-three. And if Tobias has been around seven years or so, that means I spent two years in biostasis. Damn it! Between the time in biostasis and the time spent being Tobias, I lost nine fucking years."

Erik sighs. His hair is longer than he likes, and he has a full, rather scraggly beard. Rifling through the medicine cabinet above the sink, he finds a pair of small scissors and trims the beard.

After a lengthy stay in a sauna, followed by a cold shower, Erik thinks he's ready. But ready for what? What should he be doing?

Crossing the hallway to the cafeteria, Erik has a breakfast consisting of reconstituted bacon, eggs, waffles, and coffee. Halfway through the meal, he groans as he remembers the mummified pilot. *If not a grave that no one will ever find—and given that we're on top of a goddamn mountain, probably impossible to dig—what then?* Erik laughs. *If there's one thing that a mountain's got plenty of, its stone. Hell, if I can drag his sorry ass to the top of the mountain, I can build him a cairn that'd be seen for miles.*

26

After breakfast, Erik searches the kitchen for a large plastic bag. Returning to the ship's bridge, Erik slips the bag over the pilot's corpse. As he flips the bag over so the body can fall to the bottom, the left arm breaks off. Erik shivers, grabs the arm, drops it into the bag, then draws the bag shut. He's amazed how little the body weighs.

Following the route up, which Tobias took down, Erik arrives at the saddle summit shortly before noon. By late afternoon, he has covered the body and a foot on all sides of it to a depth of two feet. Looking down at it, Erik grunts. *If it's meant to be seen for miles, it needs to be bigger, lots bigger.*

By the time Erik returns to the cargo ship, the sun has set behind the next range of mountains.

After a supper washed down with a beer, Erik returns to the captain's living quarters and stretches out on the bed. Remembering the last time he lay here and his vision of seeing and talking to Tobias, Erik decides to try again. "Tobias, if you can hear me and talk to me, I want to know why you left Salem, and why we're on some goddamn mountaintop."

Tobias comes forward as if he's been waiting. "Maybe it's different with you. Maybe you understand death because you've seen it happen, and you know what to do. But Before Rebecca and Naomi died, no one had ever died.

"For the first few days, I was a mess. I could barely move, speak, or do anything.

"Miriam was devastated and took their deaths very personally. I remember her saying that she can tell how

27

long it'll take a broken bone to mend or a wound to heal, but said she had no idea how long it would take a soul to mend. Maybe that's why she was desperate to help me. Maybe she couldn't save Rebecca and Naomi but saw my soul as a patient she could save."

Erik nods, "That sounds like Jenny."

"Silas Windcatcher, the Chief Elder, his response was to keep everyone busy and focused on what he thought was important—their jobs and responsibilities—and treat Rebeca and Naomi's deaths as a wasteful and un-wanted distraction.

"Micah Skylark, the High Priest, I remember, looked terrible. After Rebecca and Naomi's death, I don't think he slept until after the Ceremony of Remembrance and Release he cobbled together four days after their deaths.

"Even after the Ceremony, some people avoided me as if death was contagious and I was infected. Or maybe they avoided me because I was a constant reminder of something they wanted to forget.

"If that wasn't bad enough, Micah claimed he had a dream sent by God, telling him that since I was alone, without a wife or a child to love and care for, my man-ly passions would overwhelm my common sense, rea-son, and fear of God. He claimed that through me, evil would enter into the hearts and minds of the people of Salem, something he wasn't going to let happen no matter what it took."

Erik interrupts. "Just before Jenny and I left to come here, I had a dream where I was fishing in a pure moun-tain lake when a colorful dragon came out of the water and flew straight at me shooting fire which didn't burn me, but coated me in a thick layer of blackness. I couldn't move or speak. Which," Erik pauses then quietly mumbles, "is what my life has been like these past nine years."

Tobias continues as if he didn't hear. "Then Micah came up with a crazy plan to lock me up and only let me out to be used as a beast of burden. When Miriam told me what Micah intended to do, I fled Salem and escaped into the wilderness. Micah and several men chased after me. I was on foot while they were on horseback, and yet for two days I kept ahead of them until they caught up with me sitting on the bank just above the Red River with a sprained ankle. Instead of allowing myself to be captured, I rolled a log into the river, jumped on, and paddled across. As I was escaping, Micah shot an arrow that hit my backpack instead of killing me, and I was stung by some unseen monster in the river. When I got to the far side, I was safe but in awful shape."

Tobias then relates the events leading up to the canyon ordeal and his journey to the wrecked cargo ship. He finishes by saying, "It's only through God's love and benevolence that I survived hanging onto the cliff face and being nearly struck by lightning."

Erik laughs. "I don't think God had much to do with it. You still don't get it. The God you believe in is a lie. Seven years ago, you weren't created by God. Seven years ago, I arrived on this planet. My mind was programmed with memories that created you and at the same time erased all my memories of Earth. Somehow the combination of the lightning strike and the jolt of seeing Andrew and finding the commemorative coin enabled me and my memories of Earth to break through."

Tobias speaks as if each word hurts to pronounce. "If I wasn't created, am I even real?"

"You exist as a part of me."

Tobias asks, "So what happens now? I still want to live."

"I don't know. All I'm sure of is I don't belong here. I belong in a world of interstellar spaceships, not a world of horses, bows and arrows, and obsidian knives."

. . .

The next morning, as Erik eats breakfast, he remembers last night's conversation with Tobias and wonders what he would say if Tobias asked why he came to this world. How far back would he begin? Would he talk about the environmental disasters that spurred people into space or the harsh economic conditions that prompted him to jump at a chance—even one as a first-generation colonist, which comes with a forty-percent death rate in the first five years—to get off-world?

Erik chuckles silently. Does it even make sense to think of us as two distinct people? Isn't the only difference between me and Tobias the time missing from the other's memories? And the way he continues to remember more of Tobias's life, the distinction is rapidly becoming blurred.

Erik is startled by Tobias asking, "Why did you leave Earth?"

"I didn't know you could come forward unless I invited you, but I guess it doesn't matter. I'm getting used to the idea that, for now, you exist as an independent part of me. But you better get used to the idea that we can't continue like this for long before we go crazy. Eventually, one of us has to go."

Erik pushes away some reconstituted blueberry yogurt. "I didn't think possible for anything to taste that bad. "When I was eight, my mother died and my father became an abusive drunk. Grandfather Miles took me in and raised me. He was a kind and gentle man. He taught me to work stone and wood and live off of what the forest provides. It was he that taught me how to think for myself instead of depending on technology.

"After my grandfather died, I decided I had two choices: get off-world, or hole up in grandfather's cabin and become a hermit. But after six months of living alone, I decided, like it or not, I need people, so I had to find a way off-world. But getting off-world costs more than most people make in a lifetime. For many, the only way off-world is to sign themselves into what amounts to slavery for up to thirty years."

Tobias asks, "So what happened?"

"I met Jenny, and through her, I found out about the Eden Project, sponsored by a back-to-nature group called the Gimli Foundation. The project sounded ideal. They claimed to have found an uninhabited planet with such a scarcity of natural resources that it can't sustain a highly developed technological society, but would be perfect for folks willing to work hard and return to our ancient roots as farmers and herdsmen. What clinched the deal for me was a clause in the contract that after five years, anyone who wished to leave would be given free transportation to any nearby colony, or if they chose to stay, they would share in the colony's profits."

Tobias laughs, "And I've been around for just over seven years, which means they lied."

"You've no idea how much. When I signed up, I knew living conditions would be primitive, but it never occurred to me we wouldn't have electricity, computers, motorized vehicles, or be cut off from off-world contact. I figured life would be laid back and simple, not barely a step up from living like an animal."

Tobias looks around the cafeteria. "All this technology might make life easier, but it's so unnecessary. Salem's an amazing place. It's a tight-knit community that…"

Erik scoffs, "That kicked you out, not because of anything you did, but because of what they thought you might someday do. And this Rebecca, who's she? Did we ever know her before you and she were suddenly a couple? Did you love her because you and she chose each other, or did you love her because of your programming? Don't you get it? Nothing about that place is real. Your whole life is a goddamn lie."

Erik clears away his dishes, then grabs hold of the table's rim. A column of purple light appears. Speaking slowly and precisely, "Earth news, off-world colony, Eden Project."

The column of light swirls and changes into a disembodied, floating head of a beautiful blonde woman. "Seventeen videos contain both Eden and Project in the title and over five hundred million videos reference Lionel Rutger."

"Play the earliest-by-date video of Eden Project."

The light blinks out, then reappears. The floating head is now of a man with short gray hair.

"Dateline: Earth, May 24, 3253…"

"Rebecca died on May 24th."

"The Twelve Star Systems are rattled by the news that Lionel Rutger, at one time reputed to be the third-richest man in the Twelve Star Systems, died today. His body was identified by DNA and bionic implant numbers."

Erik shouts, "What's that bastard got to do with this?"

"Investigations are underway to understand how and why Lionel Rutger faked his death five years earlier. At that time, four worlds' economies were disrupted when it was discovered his immense fortune was gone. Sister Cynthia Anderson…"

"Jenny's sister?"

"…. a novice nurse's assistant at the Saint Raphael Charity Hospital in south Chicago, made the preliminary identification from the iconic photograph showing Lionel Rutger standing on the deck of his space-dome house overlooking the rings of Saturn."

"Poor kid. Jenny was supposed to be her ticket off-world, once she got established as a doctor."

"... Rutger was admitted to the hospital under the name Amos Samuels and had been living as a homeless vagrant for the last four years. Sister Cynthia claims Lionel Rutger used every penny of his fortune to finance the Eden Project."

"What the fuck?"

The cold, sterile voice continues, "...no records of such a project exist; however, Sister Cynthia claims that during his final minutes of life, Lionel Rutger eagerly talked about the Eden Project as such an enduring act of good work that God might forgive him for all the evil and suffering he caused and grant him a reprieve from the torments of hell. To carry out this plan..."

"Damn it! I've heard enough."

Tobias says, "I haven't let it keep going."

"...the 4-a rating refers to a habitable planet that lacks sufficient resources to support a profitable, self-sustaining colony. He then recruited four hundred individuals, each chosen for their genetic diversity and physical and mental health, to perform specific occupations. To abolish greed, jealousy, bigotry, racism, class, and social distinctions, the colonists were instilled with a single set of moral and ethical values, outlined in a book he called the *Holy Book of Life*..."

"That's the book you..."

"Shut up! I want to hear!"

"...based upon the apocryphal One Hundred Lost Sermons of Jesus. Furthermore, to ensure that neither the authority of these scriptures nor God's existence could ever be challenged, all memories of life on Earth were erased. False memories of being created by God and seeing and hearing God were implanted in their minds."

"That's what you were saying."

"...no contamination from Earth ever occurred. Lionel Rutger erased all information about the Eden Project, including the colony's existence and location. Lionel Rutger's greatest hope was that given a chance to live in paradise, people would thrive forever in peace, harmony, and beauty. According to Sister Cynthia, her sister Jenny Anderson and her sister's boyfriend, Erik Thorson, was selected..."

"How about that? I made planetary news."

"Now, claiming to know the truth, Sister Cynthia has been pressuring the Department of Colonization to locate the planet and prepare a rescue mission. No independent confirmation of the Eden Project has been found, and according to Margaret Whitcomb, spokesperson for the Department of Colonization..."

Erik chants, "Blah, blah, blah, blah, blah, blah, blah!"

"...as fresh developments emerge..."

"Yeah, right." Erik touches the table's rim, and the column of light disappears.

After a lengthy pause, Tobias says. "There might be no record of this colony, but somebody must have missed this cargo ship. Won't they come looking for it and then find Salem?"

"If someone were looking for this shit pile, they'd have found it by now. And unless you knew to look for it, a stone age settlement of a few hundred people would be nearly impossible to find."

Erik returns to the ship captain's living quarters and dresses in his cold-weather gear. He tosses food packets, a couple of water bottles, and a bottle of Lionel Rutger's private stock into a backpack, then stomps up the saddle between the highest peaks, determined to finish work on the cairn.

By sundown, Erik's frenzied efforts have resulted in a cairn six feet high. He slides down in the cairn's lee, and after a large swig of Scotch, asks Tobias, "Do you think it's possible to ever return to Salem?"

"After all this, I don't see how."

"Then I guess we'll become what I wanted to avoid, a hermit," another swig, "unless I can wake up Jenny and remind her it's me she loves."

"Now you're the one who doesn't get it. Me, Jenny, Rebecca, every one of the Four Hundred, believes that God created our perfect mate, especially for us. There's no way you could ever convince Jenny to leave Asher or be unfaithful to him. Who can argue with God? Besides, Asher's a good man, a carpenter; you'd like him." After a pause interrupted by two more swigs, Tobias asks, "If you had a chance to return to Earth, would you?"

"No. There's nothing there for me."

"Can you see your home star from here?"

"I have no idea where here is, so I can't say. But if we could, it'd be an average bright yellow star, like..."

Tobias looks where Erik is pointing and says, "That star is the Yellow Eye of the constellation 'the Great Bull.'"

"What an odd name."

"The star's official name is 'Still Point' because it's the point around which all the other stars appear to rotate, but I call it 'the Yellow Eye of the Great Bull' because of a dream I had just before I fled Salem. In the dream, Rebecca, Naomi, who appeared as a full-grown woman, and I were in Town Square Park in Salem when a giant white bull with one red eye and one yellow eye appeared and scooped up Micah Skylark, the High Priest, the man responsible for me leaving Salem, between his massive horns and tossed him in a river. Then Rebecca and Naomi disappeared into the bull's yellow eye. The bull then knelt, and I climbed on its back, and the bull started flying. Eventually, he landed at the Leaving Tree, a place very special to Rebecca and me. I got off the bull, and the bull started flying again, and when he was almost out of sight, he exploded into twenty stars, the yellow eye replacing Still Point. Since the dream, not only have I called that star, the Yellow Eye, but I have believed it to be the home of God. Not God's literal home, I know, because it is written in the *Holy Book of Life* that stars are balls of burning gas; still, it's a place I always know where it is, whether or not I can see it, and I know you'll think I'm dumb for saying this, but believing that God's there brings me comfort. It's a place I can focus my attention, instead of just talking to the air."

Erik takes another swig. "No, I don't think you're dumb for believing it. In fact, I wish I had something like that to believe in back on Earth. Still, I'll never get used to two moons."

"What about the ceremony you wanted to give the pilot?"

Erik shrugs. "I don't know enough about him to do him justice. We only were together that one time when we got wasted. Although, come to think of it, Andrew Last-Name-Unknown is lucky in some ways. He's remembered on three worlds. As long as we live, he'll be remembered on this planet. No doubt, there are people on Earth who remember him. And he'll be remembered by his wife and daughter, who are living somewhere in the Cygnus Quadrant.

"But on Earth, nobody knows you, and on Eden, nobody knows me. And if we die alone, it won't be long before we're completely forgotten."

Erik takes a final swig, then shatters the bottle against the cairn.

• • •

The next morning, Tobias wakes wanting to punch Erik for breaking the bottle against the cairn, but thinks, *What's the use? I'd only be hitting myself. Besides, what does it matter? How many years would it take for a single shard to wash out of the Forbidden Mountains somewhere someone from Salem could find? And by then, the glass would be so worn, no one would recognize it for what it is. Still, Erik didn't need to do it.*

Tobias growls, "Come on, Erik; wake up! "The dream last night, do you remember it?"

Erik mumbles, "Of course, after all, it was my dream."

"No, it was our dream. So tell me what you remember."

"I'm somewhere, maybe here, looking into the night sky. A light is moving toward me. I realize it's a star voyager spaceship. As it gets closer, the spaceship becomes smaller and smaller until it becomes so small it flies into my left eye. Then I grow roots, a trunk, branches, and become a tree covered in leaves. On the east side, all the apples are red, and on the west, all the apples are yellow. So, I suppose you're going to tell me what it means."

Tobias says, "Maybe. I think the dream is about us transforming into something vital, alive, and growing that ultimately bears fruit. What that means I don't know, since being alone, it's unlikely we'll ever have children. But the part about the spaceship flying into the left eye might mean that I have to accept your past, just as you must accept that you must put down roots and become a part of this world."

"So, what do you propose?"

"About a week's walk east is a large lake not far from a red sandstone tower. I've begun to build a home in an overhang on its northern shore. The lake is in the midst of a heavily forested area filled with all manner of game. Just below the Red Tower is a warm spring-fed pool that feels so good."

Erik mumbles, "Shit, why not? What else we got to do?"

Halfway down the ridge leading back to the wrecked cargo ship, Erik comes forward. "Maybe, if you take time to look close, you might find something in the cargo hold that might make Salem's people take you back."

Tobias snarls. "Don't be an idiot. No matter what we take, there'd be questions we couldn't answer without revealing the truth. It's bad enough that I know God is a lie, but if all of Salem knew, I can't imagine anything good coming of it. Besides, they're not only surviving but thriving quite nicely and will continue to thrive quite nicely without it. How can you miss something you never knew existed?"

Erik sighs. "You're right. From what I've learned from your memories, Salem is far from perfect, but what they have is worth protecting, even if it means we can't ever return."

The next morning, as Tobias prepares to leave the cargo ship, he remembers the dirty rags he arrived wearing and his promise to take nothing he didn't have when he came. "All right, Erik, maybe you're right. Maybe it won't hurt to take some things like clothes, food packets, a backpack, and something to carry water, but no gadgets or modern technology. And once we get where I left my backpack, we'll destroy everything we took."

Erik says nothing, but wonders if doing even this is too much. *Once Tobias starts making exceptions, will there be an end to what he can justify?*

A few hours later, Tobias stops atop Burial Cairn Ridg long enough to gather all the broken bottle pieces and place them in a plastic bag that he weighs down with stones and tosses over the cliff. Looking west toward the next mountain range, Tobias tries to remember how many days he's been here. Four? Five? Certainly no more than five, and yet in that time, so much has happened.

Tobias pivots and looks to where he knows the Yellow Eye, if not obscured by the sun's glare, must be and laughs. "I arrived here, not just believing in You, Old Friend, but expecting to meet You here. And now I leave having discovered you are not just a lie, but a deliberate deception devised to control my thoughts and actions so a scared old man can die believing he's escaped hell." Staring down the path he'll take, Tobias sighs, "I leave here as a man without a God or a people. I leave as a man who has awakened to his true, badly flawed nature. I leave here with little hope. I leave here staring into long, empty years of surviving but not really living. My life will be little better than an animal. Little better than the life Micah envisioned for me."

Tobias scoots and slides down the scree, keeping ahead of the thickening clouds that by evening open into a steady drizzle. He spends a cold, damp night beneath a tree that overshadows one boulder, in the natural labyrinth of stones he had named the Circle of Stones, where he spent his first night after the canyon ordeal. But because of the rain, he can't build a fire until morning.

The morning breaks with a bright blue sky. Tobias wakes, feeling like Erik feels after drinking too much, and growls at the world scrubbed clean by last night's rain.

Erik, slow to awake, says, "I've been thinking, the lower peak on the south side of the saddle, we should name Mount Andrew, and the higher peak to the north, Star Voyager Peak."

"No. No place shall have a person's name. Instead, let's name the lower peak, Pilot's Peak, which will both honor Andrew and give a person pause as they ask, what pilots their life? What is it that determines their life course? Is it God or fate or something else? And the peak to the north? No name occurs to me, but it certainly shouldn't bear the name of something that shouldn't be known."

"Whatever, this is your world, not mine."

"No, this world is just as much yours as it is mine. It's where you live, and most likely will die."

The next day, they leave the Forbidden Mountains and proceed south across the White Mesa, which abuts against them. Arriving a couple of hours before sunset at its south-facing escarpment overlooking the Red River, a short distance east of its canyon, Tobias points towards the east-south-east. "This is the Great Valley, and Salem's more than a hundred miles away."

"So what makes the Great Valley so great? It doesn't look like much except a big, flat, grassland."

Tobias smiles. "You'd be surprised. Within a day's ride is found everything the people of Salem need to live."

Erik points west, "So the place we're going to get your backpack is close by?"

"I'd guess an hour walk once we get off the mesa."

"I should have said something before we left the cargo ship, but I was afraid that you'd have left everything behind if I did." Erik groans. He finds remembering what he'd rather forget tiring. "In the decades before our first mining colonies, Earth was running out of resources, so garbage dumps became our new mines. We found ways to melt down and reuse every scrap of metal, rubber, and plastic into a nearly indestructible material that can be stamped, woven, and molded into almost everything. The clothes you're wearing will outlast us. No, the best you can do is bury everything or return it to the cargo ship."

Waking with the sun and anxious to retrieve his backpack and leave a place full of bad memories, Tobias skips breakfast and quickly descends the slope. As he passes through rows of steeply tilted hogbacks, each hogback slightly higher than the one before, he slows his pace until finally he stops and drops to his knees in front of the narrow slit where, just before the start of the Canyon Ordeal, he sheltered three nights while waiting for the rain to stop. He crawls into the slit and rubs his fingers across letters he had pecked into the rock, then obliterated in a fit of rage.

Although Erik doesn't have to ask because with a little effort he remembers, it's obvious Tobias needs to talk, so he asks, "What happened here?"

"The last night I spent here, before the Canyon Ordeal, was actually the third night I was here. From the moment I got here, it was raining. To fight the boredom of inactivity the first day, I slept as much as I could. The second day, whenever the rain let up I scrounged for tubers, berries, mushrooms, anything I could add to my food supply. But the third day, with nothing to do, I stewed in frustration and anger at God for taking Rebecca and Naomi and at Micah for making me flee Salem. Without thinking, I picked up a cobble and hammered into the back of the overhang the letters R, E, and B. When I realized what I was doing, I yelled, 'Everything always circles back to Rebecca,' and exploded. I took the cobble I had been using to peck the letters and used it to obliterate them completely, smashing my fingers a half dozen times in the process, which only made me angrier.

"Then I heard a voice, Rebecca's voice. She said, 'Tobias, God cannot live in a heart filled with anger. You'll live deaf, blind, and dumb to what it means to be alive. And we shall never find our rest.'

"You see, the people of Salem believe that when a person dies, their spirit goes to reside in God's presence. That's what the Ceremony of Remembrance and Release is supposed to do. It begins by honoring the person's life by remembering the impact the person had on those around them; then, as a penultimate act of love, each person is asked to let go and release the person's spirit so it can begin its journey to God. But here, Rebecca was telling me that because I hadn't been able to let go, their spirits were trapped in limbo between two worlds.

"So I ran to the top of the hogback, where I immediately became soaked, and I burst into sobs that nearly tore my chest apart. Then I said, 'Rebecca, Naomi, in my selfish desire to keep you close, have I prevented your spirits from entering God's presence? If so, please forgive me. There was nothing I wouldn't have done for you when you lived. Why should now be any different? Rebecca, Naomi, fly into God's presence and life everlasting, and where, perhaps one day, sooner rather than later, you wait to welcome me home.'

"As soon as I spoke those words, I felt a peace of mind and decided the best thing I could do is return to Salem and do whatever is necessary to win back my place. But then the next day, I entered the Forbidden Mountains, and, well, you know the rest."

Erik says, "I never knew Rebecca, so I can't feel her loss the same way you do, but I know how much you loved her. Is there anything of hers in the backpack?"

"No. When I left Salem, I took one of her lavender-scented handkerchiefs, a couple of hair ties, the last skein of yarn she made, and a note in her handwriting. But the night I camped at Red Bear Rock, I got careless and forgot to keep my backpack close. In the morning, I discovered my backpack ravaged, probably by pack rats. Everything inside was gone. I yelled and beat my hand against a tree until it bloodied itself. I spent hours looking but never found them."

Tobias changes into clothes from his original backpack, then slips it on his back. Staring at the backpack he brought from the cargo ship, he thinks, *If it'll never rot away, I can't just bury it and take the risk that someday it might be found.* He growls, then picks it up by one strap and starts to walk away, then stops and turns back. *This place needs a name.*

He speaks aloud, "Cold, wet, anger, frustration, pain..." then grins, "...release, because here I released Rebecca's and Naomi's spirit to return into God's presence." *Or did I? All I can be sure I did was stop wallowing in self-pity and come to terms with a future without them.* He looks to the Red River Canyon and back at the slit. *It's more than that. At the Red Bear, I was forced to let go of Rebecca's physical reminders, but here, I was stripped of everything I possessed except the clothes I wore.* "I shall call this place 'the Cave of Loss and Release.'"

From the Cave of Loss and Release, Tobias walks quickly and confidently, stopping at the base of one of the thousand-foot sandstone pillars that flank the canyon's entrance. Here, Tobias kneels and picks up a handful of gravel, which he sorts through until he holds a few small shiny flakes.

Erik asks. "Gold? It was gold that lured you into the canyon? If there's enough gold that you can find it just lying about, no wonder God called these mountains the Forbidden Mountains."

"No, even if Salem's people found the gold, it'd take years, maybe centuries, before they'd understand its properties or use. No, it's more likely these are called the Forbidden Mountains because of the wrecked cargo ship."

After scattering the gold flakes, Tobias announces, "The pillars that mark the boundary between the Great Valley and the Forbidden Mountains, I name the Pillars of..." After taking a long pause to think, he continues, "...Disobedience and Discovery. Because it is through disobedience to God's commandment that I discovered my true self."

By nightfall, Tobias has returned to the top of the White Mesa.

• • •

After two long days of walking north-east, Tobias arrives at the eastern edge of the White Mesa and camps where the river flowing into the lake north of the Red Tower tumbles down in three distinct falls. He wonders how long it has been since he last camped here and realizes he no longer knows the day's number, or even its name, but guesses the summer equinox must be within the next few days.

That night, waking to the smell of burning sulfur, Tobias watches ribbons of red, blue, yellow, and green light move in waves across the sky.

Erik asks, "What's that?"

"I don't know. I've never seen or smelled anything like it."

"On Earth, we get something similar we call the northern lights. Some people claim they can smell them, but not anything like this. I wonder if maybe this is what made the cargo ship crash."

They watch the lights until morning. As the lights disappear with the rising sun, Tobias points and yells, "There! Do you see it? That's where we're going. That's the Red Tower."

Erik says nothing.

As they are climbing down the steep talus, Erik says, "Wait! What's that?"

Tobias picks up three chalk balls of different sizes and cleans them off against his pants to reveal three equally spaced bulging eyes and two rows of jagged teeth. "I don't know. I've never seen them before."

"On Earth, we call things that were once alive and turned to stone fossils. Whatever they are, these things may be millions of years old and probably lived in an ocean that once was here."

Tobias chuckles. "Of course, I get it. In the third section of the *Holy Book of Life*, having to do with the natural history of the universe, it says that all the plants and animals on Eden evolved over unimaginably long periods, except people and the domesticated plants and animals, which were created on the Final Day of Creation. Now I understand! People and the domesticated plants and animals came from Earth. And if someday some curious person started wondering why there are no fossils of people, cows, or horses, they'd not only know why, but it'd reinforce their belief in God."

Mid-afternoon, two days later, Tobias walks along the north side of the Red Tower and trails his hand across its side as if greeting an old friend. He walks to the warm spring-fed pool surrounded by lush grass and tall trees, sloughs off his backpack, and strips.

Looking at his reflection in the pool, Tobias realizes he's never gone so long since he shaved or had Rebecca cut his hair, and he's surprised by how much weight he's lost. He takes a long thin obsidian blade out of the backpack and resharpens it. Then, where the water emerges from the pool, he kneels, shaves, and cuts his hair as short as possible without shaving his head. "Well, what do you think?"

Erik says, "I like us better with more hair. But then, not being able to keep it as clean and combed as I'd like, it's better this way."

Tobias returns to the pool, walks to its center, and stretches out. The water just covers his body, and by tilting his head slightly back, Tobias can just keep his nose out of the water. An hour after he drifts into sleep, Tobias wakes remembering a dream. He is standing on top of the Red Tower. A crow transforms into a man. The man walks to the edge of the tower and, using a fishing pole, casts an impossibly long line over the edge. He immediately catches something fighting and pulling, trying to yank the man off the edge. But the man will not be moved or give up. Finally, the man gives a great tug, and what the man has caught comes flying up. What the man has caught is the sun!

As Tobias sits up, he sees the sun seeming to rest on top of the Red Tower like a yellow flame on a giant red candle. In the sun's glare, he sees a man walking toward its edge.

Still wet, Tobias doesn't dress. Instead, he rushes to the Red Tower's base, and with the confidence that comes from hanging two days onto a cliff face, climbs.

• • •

In a half hour, Tobias has scrambled the hundred and fifty feet to the Red Tower's flat, nearly circular top. Standing in the center, he slowly pivots and thinks, *On the ground, a hundred and fifty feet is nothing. I can walk that far in less than a minute. But a hundred and fifty feet above the ground, everything's different. Not only can I see farther, but the wind is from a different direction and blowing at a different speed. And the stars*—he reaches out his right hand toward the Yellow Eye, just emerging out of the deepening twilight—*seem close enough to grasp.* But when he closes his hand, pulls his arm back, and slowly spreads open his fingers, he reveals nothing.

Tobias walks to the edge of the Red Tower and laughs. "How foolish of me to come here and not bring my fishing pole." He pantomimes the action of the man he saw fishing for and catching the sun. After miming catching the sun, Tobias drops his arms to his side, and his face goes blank. He thinks aloud, "I am the Sunfisher. I climbed the Red Tower. There is nothing I cannot do."

To prove it, Tobias lifts his right leg and starts to step forward, when a gust of wind blows him off balance. The desperate struggle to remain upright wakens Tobias to where he is and what is happening. He leaps back from the edge and crawls to the center, where he sprawls, face down, breathing hard. He lies unmoving as a fast-moving storm blows past, tossing lightning bolts but producing no rain.

Pushing himself up onto his hands and knees, Tobias stares at the place he had nearly stepped off. *What just happened? I know the difference between dreams and what is real. How could I be so foolish to think I can walk on air? Of course, two individuals vying for one mind might be enough to make me...*

Erik yells, "Crazy! Goddamn fucking crazy! That's what you are. What the hell were you thinking? You almost killed us. From now on, I'm in charge."

Tobias shrugs and says in a flat tone, "It's too dark to climb down. And even if it wasn't, I'm not sure I can trust myself to make it safely down."

"Well, I sure as hell can't make the climb, light or no light. We're trapped here until morning."

Luna has set and Selene is not far behind as Tobias lies looking up at the stars, trying to make sense of everything that had to happen to bring him to this moment. Could he, he wonders, at some point, have just said no? Or was his every decision, every choice, every action inevitable? Does anything he thinks or does matter?

All night, his mind wrestles with different possibilities. All end badly.

Waking tired, Tobias once more pivots about the center of the Red Tower. He looks to the spot in the sky where he knows the Yellow Eye—though it may not be God's home, still the point about which the universe appears to rotate—lies hidden by the brilliant blue sky. "I have no proof that God, any god, exists, but I want someone to exist. I want there to be someone who I can find comfort in talking to. I want there to be someone who cares whether I live or die. I want to believe that everything beginning with Erik's decision to leave Earth isn't the result of blind chance but has meaning. I

want to believe that all I've suffered has had a purpose—
that it's all a part of some grand plan.

"I know that neither the people of Salem nor I belong to this world, but when I came alive, and Erik disappeared, I found joy and happiness in believing I saw
and heard God, of being part of a community, and in
knowing that death is not final. However, since awakening to remembering Erik's past, I know that Salem's
God never existed. On Earth, Erik never found a reason
or the faith to believe in God. But I know the joy of
believing and want to share in that joy again.

"But if You do exist, I've yet to feel Your presence.
Perhaps I survived the canyon ordeal because You
needed me to survive, or maybe I survived by my arms'
strength and a determination to live. I don't know, but
I want to know.

"As the first person of this world to know that the
God of Salem is a lie and wonder if You exist, I ask You
to make Your presence known and reveal what You
require of me."

Tobias draws his legs in and crosses them. Sitting
with his back straight, he closes his eyes, breathes deeply
and calmly, and waits.

As the sun reaches its zenith, Erik comes forward.
"Enough foolishness. It's getting hot. I'm thirsty and
hungry and we're starting to burn in places seldom exposed to the sun. Whoever or whatever you were hoping would answer had their chance and chose not to
show. Now let's get off this damn rock before things
get bad."

"Perhaps you're right. Once down on the ground and dressed, I can try again. There's no reason to expect Someone will or should answer the first time I ask." Tobias stretches, stands, then walks to the place along the edge where he climbed up last evening. He traces an easy route with his eyes, but then wobbles. His legs grow weak and his eyes blur, the ground rising, falling, and spinning about him. He drops to his knees and closes his eyes. Tobias crawls to the center of the tower.

Erik yells, "What the fuck!"

"I don't know."

"Without food or water, we sure as hell can't stay here, and the longer we do, the harder it'll be to get down. Rest a few minutes and then try again."

An hour before sunset, Erik yells, "We must go before it gets too dark to climb down."

Tobias whispers, "No. Someone wants us to stay."

"What? You thought it was crazy when you almost tried to walk on air—well, this is even crazier. One day without water is bad. Three days without water will kill us."

Tobias whispers, "I know," then curls into a ball.

Erik laughs. "If you think it hurts now, wait until the next day, and the next day." Just before he withdraws, Erik thinks, *If someone's going to suffer, it'll sure as hell won't be me.*

The second day, the hottest day of the year, Tobias's lips crack, his tongue swells, his throat burns, and his skin blisters. By mid-afternoon, he tries to think through his pain and suffering and remember what life was like with Rebecca as they lived and loved in Salem, but he can't, his entire attention instead taken up by pain. He thinks, *This is how it has always been and always will be—constant, eternal torment.*

A dozen crows land on the edge of the Red Tower and busily strut. Thankful for the distraction, Tobias watches as they take flight and circle higher and higher until they are nearly out of sight. Then, one after another, they fold their wings and playfully dive straight down until leveling out. Over and over, the crows continue their game until twilight.

Unable to make any sound, Tobias thinks, *Someone, if I die, will it be a good death, a meaningful death, or shall I die alone and forgotten, my body carrion for the crows?*

The third day, as his body shuts down, Tobias sucks on a small pebble to try to produce moisture. His hunger is gone, his body cannibalizing itself. He no longer tries to sit up but remains curled in a ball.

Erik comes forward. "You goddamn fucking bastard! Is this how we're going to die? Why the hell did you ever wake me? If you hadn't, I would have died a peaceful death, without ever knowing I had lived!"

Tobias drifts in and out of consciousness. Just before sundown, a black wall of clouds rolling along the ground racing toward the Red Tower hits him with a blast of sand-filled wind that fills his eyes and nose and batters his blistered skin.

Within his mind, Tobias whispers, "Rebecca? Naomi?"

They are standing in a beautiful meadow filled with flowers of every color and alive with birds and butterflies of every description. They are smiling and waving for him to join them. Then, moving without moving, Tobias is with them. He is no longer hungry, thirsty, or in pain. He is strong and alive and runs to meet them. Just as they are about to touch hands, he is startled by a raspy screech. The meadow, Rebecca, and Naomi vanish.

A half-dozen crows are strutting nearby.

"Is he a groundling?"

"He looks like a groundling."

"What's a groundling doing here?"

Tobias, not surprised he can understand the crows, answers. "I came here looking for something."

"There's nothing here to be found."

"I came looking for God, and to understand how to live my life."

All the crows but one take flight. The crow that's left transforms into a man. Tobias writhes as he watches the man fish for and catch the sun.

A clap of thunder announces the beginning of a downpour. Tobias opens his mouth. A few life-giving raindrops slither down his throat in excruciating pain. The rain lasts only a few minutes, but enough has fallen to fill every depression on top of the Red Tower with water.

Pushing himself to his hands and knees, Tobias goes from puddle to puddle, lapping water like an animal. He stops at one puddle and, like a crow, cocks his head to one side and stares at what he's seeing. At the bottom of the puddle is a pile of blueberries. Tobias chews the berries, squeezing out every ounce of moisture before swallowing their meat.

After finishing his feast, Tobias stands, and as if in a trance, walks to the edge and begins climbing down. Every move feels like he is being supported and guided by some invisible force. On the ground once more, Tobias walks to a nearby boulder on which a crow is perched. He hoarsely whispers, "Thank you for the blueberries."

The crow ruffles its feathers.

"Why did I have to suffer so, only to have the dream in the pool repeated?"

The crow flutters up a foot before again landing.

"I no longer feel that I am Tobias or Erik, but something else and that something else needs a name. So, to honor my friends the crow, I name myself Corvus."

The crow flies off.

Tobias staggers to the shade of the trees adjacent to the pool. He removes several white starchy tubers out of his backpack, which he mushes with water into a bland, runny paste that slides easily down his throat.

It takes three days for Tobias's blisters to scab over and will take many more days before his body is functioning anything like normal.

# CHAPTER THREE

Two weeks after leaving the Red Tower, Corvus, making the final ascent by the light of a half-full Selene, stands atop of the Way Forward Mountains, two hours before sunrise. Not wanting to disturb his view of a star-filled sky by building a warming fire, he hunkers down in the lee of a large boulder.

From his backpack, Corvus removes one of three faux-leather-bound journals he took from the wrecked cargo ship. He opens it to the first still-blank page and runs his fingers across the soft, light beige paper, the same paper upon which the *Holy Book of Life* is printed. In his left hand, Corvus holds a stylus that needs no ink, only the slightest pressure, to leave behind writing that will never fade or run. After a pause to mark the solemnity of his first entry, he writes:

> Why am I doing this, when I hope these journals, detailing my lives as Tobias, Erik, and Corvus, will never be read? But then why build a cairn for Andrew? Why continue to give names to things no one will ever know? The answer must be: I do this for myself, so perhaps one day I can look back across my life's landscape and find within it purpose and meaning which presently

I'm too short-sighted to see. Perhaps, one day, I'll understand that all I've lived, loved, lost, and suffered had to happen for a reason I may not understand until death is upon me.

I have no idea of either the day of the week or the exact date. But if the first night I spent atop the Red Tower was, as I believe, the summer's solstice, then I reckon today to be 8/1/7.

—8/2/7—

Tonight, I sit upon the summit of the Way Forward Mountains awaiting sunrise. Since leaving the Red Tower, I've had a fantasy about being here and watching the sun rise on land never before seen with human eyes. And, as the land floods with light, I imagine it revealing something so amazing that it will reveal my life's direction.

It's been more than three weeks since my near-fatal fast atop the Red Tower. I began my fast expecting Someone—a new name for God—to manifest Himself. Instead, the Sunfisher appeared in a vision as I lay on the verge of death. I'm not exactly sure who or what the Sunfisher is, but I'm certain he's not God. I think he might be the person I might become, but what kind of person catches the sun?

However, since that experience, I've noticed nothing is the same. Tobias and Erik no longer exist, although their memories persist. I no longer think of myself as Erik, an alien from another planet, or Tobias, an interloper whose life was built on an illusion, but I think of myself as Corvus, the one who belongs but not to Eden, but Alura. I named the world Alura for the simple reason that I like how the name sounds like what it is: something luring me forward.

I also named the pool at the base of the Red Tower the Doorway, because whenever I lie within its waters, it's like a doorway opens and not what I want but what I need walks through. The Forbidden Mountains I renamed the Gateway Mountains because they are the gate through which I have to pass to discover my true nature. The slightly lower mountain range west of the Gateway Mountains, where I now sit, I named the Way Forward Mountains, because I believe they are my way forward to discovering my true destiny.

For most of an hour, I've watched the land below grow lighter, and haven't written anything. I know I shouldn't feel disappointed, but I am. Directly below me, the mountain ends in a reddish-purple barren looking landscape. Off to the north-west, I see two smoking mountains. Directly west, I see another faint line of mountains. To the south-west, I see an open grassland, similar to the Great Valley, and a dark green line that skirts the barren landscape, possibly a river. And if it is a river, then it must be the Red River, which would explain why it is so much larger than all the other rivers of the Great Valley. Because instead of heading in the Way Forward Mountains or the Gateway Mountains, it begins in some distant place, where one day, when I feel more confident of my ability to survive, I must go.

Although I am disappointed no place called to me, I am not deterred from going forward and making this new land my home.

As Corvus continues watching light stream into the lands stretching below the mountains, he muses. *What is it I'm looking for when I say I'm looking for a place to call home? A place of abundance, where life is easy? A place I feel close to God? Or is the idea of finding God something that should be left behind, as I left behind all the technological wonders within the cargo ship's hold, until God in whatever form reveals Himself to me? No, what I want is a place I can sink into in the same way I lie in the Doorway, wrapping me with its warmth, and revealing not what I want, but what I need. Does such a place exist? And if it does, will I ever find it? And if I find it, will I recognize it for what it is?*

—8/15/7—

I have decided to go no farther. What's the use?

In nine days, it will be exactly three months since Rebecca and Naomi died. I'm not sure what made me think of it, except maybe that now that I've arrived at the place I intend to build my house, I'm not happy.

Erik said after living as a hermit for six months, he realized he needed people to live. It hasn't even been three months, and here I'm wondering what's happening in Salem. Does anyone miss me? Or, not that it matters because how would I know, has anyone else died, so I am no longer unique? I have even caught myself imagining what I'd be doing if I was there.

The Way Forward Mountains do not extend this far south, which means only the Gateway Mountains separate me from the Great Valley. But actually, it's so much more than mountains that separate me from Salem and prevent my return.

Directly below where I'm sitting is a south-facing overhang in which I'll build a place to live, but I doubt it will ever be more than that. Below the overhang runs a river that a hundred yards east empties into an enormous lake. I am confident I'll find everything I need to survive.

But, what's so frustrating is that when I left the Red Tower a little more than a month ago, I felt enlivened, like I had been created anew and was experiencing everything for the first time. Like the world was an exciting place waiting for me to discover. But now, has anything really changed? Rivers are still rivers, trees are still trees, rocks are still rocks, and one day is like another.

Corvus returns the journal to the backpack, then, staring east into the backside of the Gateway Mountains, falls asleep and wakes to the sun shining in his eyes and the Sunfisher whispering, "Say yes to beauty, yes to tears, yes to frustration, and not knowing. Say yes to hope and sorrow, say yes to love and death, say yes to ride the Great Bull, to swim down through a river and out the other side, say yes to be a fruit-bearing tree with roots in a mountain and branches in the sky, say yes to fishing and catching the sun, say yes to life."

Corvus smiles. *At least Sunfisher has not abandoned me.*

*He said not what I wanted to hear but what I needed to hear. His message seems clear: I can live a life wallowing in what I've lost and can never have, or I can say yes and learn to live the life I'm meant to live.*

After a short climb down to the overhang, Corvus takes a stick and draws lines in the sand blown into the overhang, outlining where he'll place walls, the fire pit, and a half dozen storage areas along with rough calculations as to the amount of stone needed and the time it will take to complete.

After three weeks of steadily building dry masonry walls, he chinks with mud and straw. With autumn still two weeks away, Corvus decides to take a break and explore the lakeshore south, taking careful notes as to the location of different raw materials, such as needed to replace his bow and arrows, and all manners of edible and useful plants.

Early afternoon of the third day, Corvus arrives at a shallow, slow-moving river, the lake's southern outlet, winding through tall ancient stands of oak, maple, and ash, and decides he'll go no farther. Instead, Corvus stands unmoving, immersing himself in a soft yellowish-green light that hangs in the air like a fragrant mist illuminated by a chorus of butterflies, birds, and a hundred kinds of flowers in bloom. Then, clambering onto a fallen tree twice as tall as he stands and covered in a carpet of green moss and mushrooms, Corvus stretches out as if he's lying in the warm water of the Doorway.

The more Corvus relaxes and listens, the more the meadow comes alive with insects, birds, plants, and animals he had overlooked. He doesn't move or even flinch when a snake slithers across his chest. A deer nearly brushes his legs as she comes down to drink. He speaks to her in a small voice.

"The first time I arrived at the Red Tower, another of your kind visited me with her baby. When I saw her, I cried. After all I had suffered—the death of my mate, having to flee Salem, nearly dying as I escaped across the Red River—finding such unexpected, gentle beauty opened my heart and for the first time I didn't just think but felt how much I had lost and how alone I was. But seeing the mother and child also reminded me that if you look, love is everywhere. Since then, much has happened. Once I was known as Tobias, then I discovered I was Erik, but now I am Corvus and on my way to becoming Sunfisher."

As shadows spread across the glade, Corvus has to remind himself this is not a dream. Or is it? A brown butterfly trimmed blue with cream-colored spots along the wing's edge grazes his forehead, nose, and lips, then flitters away. Branches snap, and out of the corner of his left eye, he sees a woman with raven black hair falling past her waist. Music, like the aroma promising a beautiful meal, lures him forward. He runs after her and several times catches a glimpse before she disappears. Just when he thinks he has lost her, she appears only to disappear behind the next tree.

"Wait! Who are you?"

She smiles and waves him to follow, but he doesn't get close until she stops just across a small clearing. Corvus watches as she discards her long, thin, light blue dress trimmed with red and gestures to him to come to her. He hesitates. She is beautiful, desirable, but who is she? Where does she come from? And why is she offering herself to him? These are questions for later. Corvus hurries towards her. With each step, he sinks deeper into the mud, but the deeper he sinks, the faster he walks until he is knee-deep, no longer able to lift his leg clear.

The woman grows in size; her eyes glow red, her hands turn to claws, her mouth teems with jagged teeth. Rising, she unveils bat-like wings and swoops towards Corvus—just as a crow landing on his leg wakes him.

Corvus blinks into awareness and is surprised to discover he hasn't moved. He's still stretched out on top of the tree. Looking nervously about, Corvus wonders if instead of a dream, something in the air created his nightmarish vision.

Corvus picks up a two-foot, straight branch of ebony wood lying across his lap and turns it over to look at it from every direction, then speaks to a nearby crow. "Old Friend, thank you for waking me. If you hadn't, I wonder if I would have ever wakened. This branch, I don't remember finding it. Where did it come from? Is it, like the blueberries I found at the top of the Red Tower, a gift left by crows? Or is it a gift left by the woman I chased after? That woman? Is she a goddess or a trick of the mind? This place is dangerous. I must go before I can't."

Three days later, Corvus arrives at his home in the

overhang with a backpack filled with nuts and berries and the knowledge of where, in a month, he can harvest rice grass and collect melons, peppers, and edible tubers and roots.

For the first time since fleeing Salem, Corvus is confident he will not only survive the winter but thrive.

• • •

Following his return from the Goddess in the Ethereal Glade, Corvus works long, hard hours finishing his house, laying in firewood stores and preparing and fashioning furs and animal skins into clothes and shoes.

Only after the first snow arrives does Corvus take a moment to relax. His journal for that day begins:

—11/6/8—

Last night it snowed four inches. I am warm and well-fed. This morning I found the branch left for me, either by the crows or the Goddess of the Ethereal Glade. I shall make it into a flute. My big projects for this winter are to build a canoe and replace my bow and arrows. Work on the canoe will be sporadic, as the log I have chosen is too large and heavy to move into the overhang, so all work on it will have to be performed outside, weather permitting.

Just now, I caught myself wanting to thank Old Friend, meaning God, instead of my friends, the crows, for helping me prepare for winter, but that,

I know, would be an empty gesture. Still, I feel ungrateful for not thanking someone. But who? The question that still haunts me. Maybe, if I want someone to thank, I should thank Erik's grandfather, Miles, who taught Erik to live the way people had for thousands of years before modern technology, by living as a part of nature instead of making of nature an enemy that must be continually defeated. Perhaps Erik and Tobias were wrong. Not everything brought from Earth is bad.

Corvus wonders what happened to the flute that Erik, under his grandfather's watchful eye, carved from a giant sequoia branch and kept among his most prized possessions when he left Earth. Not only did it have a beautiful sound, but it had a carved raven that could slide forward and partially block the sound-hole to change its tonal quality. Searching through Tobias's memories, he finds nothing.

Despite his worries, winter is mild, passing quickly and easily, partly because of his work on the canoe and replacing his bow and arrows, and partly from the joy he derives from playing his flute. It surprises Corvus, the ease with which he recalls the muscle memory required to play the flute. Although he remembers tunes that Erik played, he prefers the melodies he's composed to capture some emotion or memory. But of all the melodies, including *Lament for Rebecca, Red Tower Vision, The Canyon Ordeal, The Awakening,* and others, the one to which he always returns is *The Ethereal Glade*, celebrating the home of the Goddess.

When the spring equinox dawns, the lake is free of ice, and Corvus has finished the canoe. It is twelve feet long, three feet wide, and one foot deep, with a slightly curving bottom.

After tossing his backpack into the canoe, Corvus launches it into the river's nearly nonexistent current. Hanging onto the far edge and bending low, he steps into the canoe's center and waits until he feels steady before stepping in with his other foot. Quickly pivoting in place, Corvus drops onto the seat and again waits for the rocking to cease.

For the first hour, Corvus keeps close to shore, then paddles out of the sight of land as his confidence grows. Placing the paddle in the canoe's bottom, Corvus leans back, letting the warm sun wash across his face. The lake mirrors the deep blue sky, and with no wind to stir up waves, the water rises and falls in a slow, gentle swale that lulls him into feeling disconnected from his body, like he felt atop the Red Tower when he looked down on his nearly dead body as he talked to the crows. He thinks that it's moments like this that the soul's heart and mind open and he ceases to exist.

Without realizing, Corvus falls asleep, then wakes with the sun low in the sky. He wakes, thinking, *What an odd dream.* In the dream, he was not in a canoe but sitting with his legs crossed and back straight, gently bobbing on top of the water. Just out of reach was a flame growing out of a lotus. Both he and the flame were flowing out of the lake and upstream in the river that flows beneath his home. As they passed his house, the flame opened like a water lily to reveal a beautiful butterfly. The butterfly vanished into a bright flash of light that fell like warm rain. Wherever the rain fell, new life erupted.

Reaching into the canoe's bow, Corvus takes his flute out of the backpack and, giving no thoughts to the notes, plays. As he plays, he thinks of everything wrong with the dream. *A person can't bob like a stick on water. Nothing flows upstream. Fire can't float on water. Flames can't become a butterfly. Butterflies can't explode into life-giving light. But to dwell on the impossible,* he tells himself, *is to miss the point. So what is the point?*

As he continues to play, the melody changes, until soon he is playing *The Ethereal Glade.* When he finishes, he replaces the flute into his backpack, and hesitantly turns the canoe south, traveling by moonlight and guided by starlight. When exhaustion finally overwhelms him, Corvus draws in the paddle and leans back in to sleep. In the morning, he discovers the canoe has drifted within sight of the southern shore.

Corvus hesitates to go farther. His first experience in the Ethereal Glade was beautiful, but also terrifying. But did it have to be? This time when he returns, it will be different; he won't go empty-handed but will return with the flute made from the branch the Goddess gifted him, and he'll play her a song he wrote in her honor.

Two hours later, Corvus has beached his canoe at the Ethereal Glade's entrance, leaving everything behind but his flute. Once more, he clambers on top of the fallen log, taller than himself, that he stretched out on during his first visit. He sits with his back straight and legs crossed and imagines himself bobbing on top of the lake. *The light is softer and the honey-scented perfume stronger than I remember, but just as before, everywhere I look, something is moving or in bloom.*

Without waiting for an invitation, Corvus takes up his flute and plays *The Ethereal Glade*, followed, without stopping, by the *Hymn to the Goddess*.

Thirty feet away, the Ethereal Glade shimmers, and the Goddess appears as translucent light that gathers into a body.

The Goddess smiles as she dances, twirls, and leaps. Swirling forward until her dress nearly touches the log on which Corvus is sitting, She asks, "Why did you return?"

"As soon as I return to my home, I will answer the call of a dream and follow the east-flowing river that flows beneath my house west to its source."

The Goddess stops dancing. "If you go looking for answers, you won't find any. All you can hope to find are questions."

"Then what is the point of going anywhere or doing anything?"

The Goddess laughs. "Lie back, close your eyes, and breathe deep, then tell me what you experience."

Corvus does as the Goddess requests. "I feel calm. Every sound has a taste, color, and texture. Plants, rocks, animals, trees, water, wind, everything I see swirls together, and I see myself vanishing into the swirl. Wait! What's happening? Why has the sun turned black?"

When he receives no answer, Corvus sits up. The Goddess is gone.

*What does it mean for the sun to turn black?*

—6/10/8—

When I left my home on Floating Fire Lake, I thought the journey west to the Calling River's source in the Flattop Mountains would be no more difficult than my journey from the Way Forward Mountains to my home. But two weeks into my journey, the river I followed west from my home disappeared beneath an expanse of towering sand dunes I call the Great Emptiness. During the following week, twice I went one day without water and once two days, before the river returned.

These mountains must be considerably lower than either the Gateway or Way Forward Mountains, as their flat summit is covered in a lush pine forest and dotted with innumerable lakes. Looking west, I feel an excitement I've never felt. As lush and vibrant as the Ethereal Glade is, it pales in comparison to what I see endlessly stretching out before me, so much so that I wonder if I should ever again want to endure the hardships of crossing the Great Emptiness. What, if anything, is stopping me from making this land my home? If I am never to return to Salem, does it matter if I live a hundred and fifty or three hundred miles away?

Corvus takes up his flute and plays without conscious thought. As the final note of a new melody fades, two thoughts fight for his attention. First, he names the tune *Paradise Found*, and second, a feeling that something isn't right. Again he plays the melody, but this time, he listens intently to every note he plays and notices every breath he takes. *How is it possible for the music to echo longer than it should? But more importantly, how can the last note be wrong? A trick of the mountain air?*

Corvus plays a long trill and waits. The echo is silent for a moment, but after a lengthy delay, what he played is repeated followed by a half dozen added notes. He is answered!

He plays *Lament for Rebecca*, then waits, and a different tune, similar in tone, answers back. He continues playing until Luna rises high enough to light the mountain's far side when whoever is answering falls silent.

The next day, Corvus moves only a few miles down the mountain. How far can a flute be heard in perfect conditions? Two miles? Three at the most? That night, Corvus builds a fire upon an exposed granite knob, hoping whoever answered him might be lured by the smell of a grouse slowly cooking on a makeshift spit. But when the grouse is prepared and no one has arrived, Corvus plays *Red Tower Vision* and *Hymn to the Goddess*. He sighs in relief; once again, he is answered.

Corvus, accessing Erik's memories, thinks the survey crews had to have classified the planet as uninhabited, but what was meant, as it happened on other worlds, was that no technologically advanced life forms were present—only life forms that one day might provide a source of cheap, exploitable labor. Maybe it wasn't the wreck of the cargo ship or the gold at the mouth of the Red River Canyon but the existence of these people that prompted God, or rather the company behind the planet's colonization, to name the mountains at the west edge of the Great Valley the Forbidden Mountains, thus preventing the two people, at least for a very long time, from ever meeting.

That night while awaiting sleep, Corvus imagines his unknown audience as sensuous and beautiful as the Ethereal Glade's Goddess. *And when we meet, it will be with the same—no, better than the same love I felt for Rebecca because our love will not be based upon a lie but upon a deep cosmic force resonating between us.*

The next day he travels another few miles down the mountain after gathering berries and mushrooms and snaring a rabbit in anticipation of a feast he hopes his unseen companion will share. Corvus takes time to shave, bathe, and comb out his hair, which, not having been cut since leaving the Red Tower, hangs four inches past his shoulder.

Just after sunset, Corvus plays a new song he's worked on all day called *Song of Invitation and Welcoming.* When he hears the reply, disappointment so real he can taste it presses down hard on his heart. She—it has to be she—is playing from a considerable distance.

After two days of following his unseen companion down the slope, Corvus stops inside a small clearing surrounded by towering deciduous trees. Within the clearing are a half dozen nearly identical house-sized boulders that look like they might be dice rolled in a game of chance.

*When my unseen companion understands I will go no farther, that I will not follow her indefinitely, she will have no choice but to come and reveal herself.*

The next morning, lying face down and shivering with a high fever, Corvus, doubled over in gut-wrenching pain, vomits awake. His throat is raw and inflamed. Even within the deep shade of the oaks, the sun's light burns his skin.

With the little strength he can muster, Corvus listens. The jungle is alive with birdsong, flowing water, the chattering of monkeys, and the deep, guttural growl of something dangerous circling closer. But beneath the chatter, he hears a calming footstep. "Goddess?"

# CHAPTER FOUR

Corvus startles at the sound of his voice asking, "Why is it so dark? Why is it so cold?" Instinctively, he pulls the soft, furry blanket closer and tighter. His body stiffens as the furry blanket strokes his forehead and awareness penetrates his head, exploding with pain: it's not a blanket, but a who. He whispers, "Who are you?"

"I am nobody. Your fever has broken."

"How are you talking? I hear nothing but myself."

"You hear my thoughts."

"You speak my language. How is that possible?"

"In exchange for sight, the gods gave me the gift to understand and talk to all creatures in their language."

"Where am I?"

"You are in The Healing Place. Three days ago, when I look for you, I find you dying. I bring you here."

"Three days?"

"For now, rest, food and water, but mostly rest. In two days more, you can join my people."

"I have so many questions..."

"Questions? Am I to be tested?" She places a wooden spoon against his lips. "Eat. Don't ask what. Does it matter if it makes you better?"

Corvus cleans a paste that tastes of pumpkin and avocado off the spoon, followed by something thick and sickly sweet with the texture and taste of lemon-flavored honey. His medicinal feast concludes with a sip of cold water.

• • •

How many hours passed? Without the aid of the sun, moon, or stars, Corvus has no way of knowing. "Butterfly, where are you?"

He surprises himself by calling his unseen, unknown host Butterfly, and wonders if the name is inspired by the butterfly that woke him during his second visit to the Ethereal Glade or the butterfly in his dream that emerged from the flame and exploded into life-giving rain.

"Crow, I will soon be with you. Do not be scared. You are safe."

Corvus smiles. Somehow she knows what his name refers to.

Whether he fell asleep or she moved too quietly to be heard doesn't matter. Butterfly is beside him; her too-soft hand is on his forehead. Corvus lifts the hand covered in short fur, strokes it, then places it on his cheek and sighs. She raises his hand to her face and moves it about—nose, mouth, two eyes, but the cheeks, forehead, and chin are all covered with soft fur. She then moves his hand down to her breasts. Corvus jerks his hand back when he realizes what he is touching, but she places it back and squeezes his hand. Her breasts are covered with soft fur, except for the area about the nipples.

Corvus hears a purring laugh as she places his hand onto his chest and begins stroking his body. Her touch is arousing, but is it meant to be? Or, being blind, is touch her way of seeing? She slips her hand beneath his pants' waistband, and just before she can feel how aroused he is, he stops her hand and again hears the purring laugh. Gentle, but not mocking.

"Your second-skin can come off?"

*Second-skin?* Corvus chuckles. "My second-skin I call clothes, and yes, it comes off."

"Your face was smooth when I found you, but now it's rough. I don't understand."

Corvus thinks, *How different we must be in appearance. And yet, when she saw my need, her heart opened, and she took me in.* "Whiskers. They are called whiskers, and if I don't cut them, they will continue to grow and cover my cheeks and chin."

"Like the hair on your head? It was so long to be a danger, so I cut it. Then I search for ticks and other small creatures."

Corvus rubs his hand across the top of his head. "The last time I cut my hair, I cut it much shorter."

"Then you are not mad? I did nothing wrong?"

"No, you did nothing wrong."

Although Corvus can see nothing, he feels the silent approach of another person. He hears Butterfly say, "Grandmother, he shall live."

He feels another pair of hands. These hands are strong and practical. They move across Corvus's face, then grasp his shoulders and arms uncomfortably tight. Tobias feels a soft pressure as she lays her ear on his chest. He chuckles silently. If she is trying to listen to his heart, she is listening too high and too far to the right. She then reaches down and grabs Tobias's testicles. He gasps, and she laughs. The woman Butterfly called Grandmother leaves without having said a word.

Corvus asks, "What was your grandmother doing?"

"She is everybody's grandmother, even yours. When I told Grandmother you have no heart, she said you must be a god. But how, she asked, can a god be sick?"

*A god? Is the reason she saved me because she thinks I'm a god?* "Do you think I'm a god?"

"You have no heart but have a second-skin, whiskers, speak strange words, and the thing you carried on your back, the tiny throwing sticks with feathers, the big thing with a cord, the many strange leaves with black marks all in neat rows. All so strange, but your music stick only a god or its servant may play. So then I think you must be a god. But how can you be a god Grandmother doesn't know?"

Corvus grasps her hand. What he desperately needs is a friend. Does it matter if he has to lie? Does it matter if she isn't human?

"I appear as I am to test your people to see if you will pity a stranger in need."

"When first I heard your music, I went home. The next day, I bring Grandmother. She said I must not let you find me, but I should watch and if you change shape, what animal you become. The next day I tell Grandmother you do not change, but your music is sad."

"But you're blind. How can you tell if I change?"

"Eyes are only one way to see. The next night you make the magic bloom dance in the air, so I know you are a god. I go back and tell Grandmother."

"Magic bloom?"

Without Butterfly saying a word, he sees within his mind the dancing orange flame of a campfire.

"Grandmother tells me I should bring you to her. That is when I find you almost dead. With the help of Taj-jul, I bring you here. Grandmother doesn't know what to think of you. Even now, she chews the leaves that help her move without moving to the place the gods sit in council. The headman suspects Grandmother for having me bring you here. He makes plans to test you."

"What kind of test?"

"I do not know. Why are you suddenly afraid? What's wrong?"

"Come, lay your ear on the place I show you."

Butterfly does as she is told. "I do not understand. You have a heart, but not in the right place."

Corvus lets go Butterfly's hand and turns away. "I am no god." After a long pause, and no response from Butterfly, he continues, "I have journeyed here from beyond the mountains, beyond a great emptiness, and yet another mountain." After a long pause and a deep breath, he continues. "And to that place, I came upon a shaft of starlight." How better to explain interstellar travel? "From a world like this, moving about the un-moving star."

Corvus feels Butterfly disappear into silence, until after many moments she says, "You say you are no god, then tell me of a journey only a god can make and tell me things beyond understanding. I know the star of which you speak, but how can it have a world? There is but this world, and stars are the tears cried by Magic Bloom at the beginning."

Corvus says, "Tell me."

"Why? You are a god. You were there when the stories were lived. Will you become angry and strike me down if I get the stories wrong?"

"No, my heart is filled with love, not anger. If I am a god, I am a god of love."

Butterfly is silent for a long moment. "I know many gods and have heard of others, but never a god of love. You must teach me your songs and rituals that I may teach my people."

"Please tell me the story of how your world came to be."

Butterfly's voice drops into a rhythmic chant. "Before there was everything, there was only Darkness, and Darkness was as tiny as the tiniest grain of sand. And Darkness was very cold and all alone. After a very long time, Darkness says, 'It is not right that I should be alone,' then thinks, 'but I have only thought I am alone, I have not searched to see if that is true.' So Darkness looks in every direction possible to look, and as he looks he creates an emptiness big enough to contain all that is. And within that space, Darkness found he was yet alone. He cries. His tears become the water and the land. After a long time, his tears stop. Darkness says, 'I have thought, and I have looked, but I have not reached out and felt with my hands.' And so Darkness gathers together the land and the water and fashions them into mountains and valleys and the big waters, the rivers, and lakes, and the rain that falls to nourish the land. Again, he finds he is alone, and again, he cries. This time, his tears form fragrant flowers and delicious fruit. After a long time, his tears stop, and he says, 'I have thought, I have looked, I have felt with my hands, but I have not yet smelled nor tasted.' And so he smells and tastes the fragrant flowers and delicious fruits, but again finds he is alone. This time when he cries, his tears form all the animals, the trees, and grasses.

"After a long time, he stops crying and thinks, 'What shall become of me? Must I be alone all my days?' And then he thinks, 'I have thought, I have looked, I have reached out and felt with my hands, and I have smelled and tasted, but I have not listened and is it not said that listening is the source of all wisdom?' And so Darkness listens, and after a long time, he hears crying. In his heart, he rejoices not for the sound of crying but because he knows he is not alone. And so he searches the world among the mountains and valleys, the great waters, lakes, and streams, and among the fragrant flowers and delicious fruit, the animals, trees, and grasses, and still, he cannot find the source of the crying.

"Darkness sees Magic Bloom is very beautiful, and he cannot look away from her dance. He sees that every tear she cries becomes a tiny drop of light. Darkness says to Magic Bloom, 'Why are you crying?' Magic Bloom says, 'I cry because I am alone, and it's not right to be alone.' Darkness says, 'I, too, am alone. Let us live together, and never again shall we be alone.' And Magic Bloom is happy and grows in size, brightness, and warmth, so much so that Darkness becomes afraid that she should grow so large that she would fill the space he created and leave no place for him. And Darkness says, 'Let us each fill half of the great space I have created and decree that the land and all the plants and creatures upon it shall at all times be covered half in light and half in darkness. Let us make it that all the world should know night and day; let us make the great circle spin above the land.' And so it was.

"Then Magic Bloom asks, 'What shall become of my children I cried into existence? Within my light, they shall not be seen.' Darkness says, 'Let them spread throughout the night and be called stars.' Magic Bloom says, 'When first my heart broke, I cried the biggest tear and then two smaller tears. Let the biggest tear stay in the day, for its light is the brightest of all lights, and let it be called the sun. The two smaller lights, let them move through both night and day that they might be used to count the days and years, and these we shall call moons.'

"Then, after all was done, as was spoken, Darkness and Magic Bloom lay together in perfect union, no longer able to tell where one ended and the other began. From their union came many children, each child a god, except the last two children were no gods—they were the first two people. Darkness and Magic Bloom spoke to the first two people. 'Because you are created last, you are the least of our creation, and because you are the least of our creation, you must one day die. And because you must one day die, we give you the gifts of thought and wisdom that you may know the will of the gods and learn to honor and obey them with your every thought and action and reap the reward of joy and happiness all your days.'

"Is this the story your people tell?"

Corvus shakes his head. "I know many stories about how the world came to be, but believe none. Your story is good because it teaches that it's not good to be alone. It teaches that it is good to be part of a community."

"Are your people many in number?"

"Including children, we are more than eight hundred."

"I don't know such a number."

Corvus closes his eyes and pictures the luncheon in Town Square Park in Salem following the Ceremony of Remembrance and Release for Rebecca and Naomi. He feels Butterfly enter his mind.

"Your people are more than all the Seven Tribes. Why have you left your people and come here?"

"During our journey to this world, my people slept. When we awoke, we had forgotten everything about the world from which we came. When we awoke, my people were tricked into believing we had never lived. We were tricked into believing that we saw and heard God speak out of a magic bloom that constantly changed color and gave off no heat. And after God finished speaking, God left. But, that we might remember Him, God left behind many of the strange leaves covered with marks in rows, that we might know the rules we must follow."

Butterfly says, "I feel sorry for your people. How can it be that your God left? Everywhere I look, I see gods."

"My people do not live together in one big place as do your people, but each person and their mate has their own house made of rock and mud with a roof made of branches covered with mud and grass. We raise many kinds of animals, so we do not hunt. Some animals we raise for meat, some for eggs, some for milk, some to ride upon and carry heavy loads. We grow many plants in fields. We never lack for food."

"Show me."

Corvus closes his eyes and imagines himself walking through Salem. Once again, Butterfly enters his mind.

"So many paths, all straight. So many corners. People live close but apart. The animals I do not know, but they do not look happy. They cannot freely move.

"Why would people who can travel on starlight live like this? I look, but I see no gods."

"My job was to gather and shape stone and build a house for God."

"You have only one God who left, yet you build a house for Him to live in? Why would your God stay there?"

"My mate made threads from animals' hair, which my people sew together to make our second skins."

"All your people wear second skins?"

"Yes. Women are careful to keep their breasts covered so men don't lust after women who are not their mates."

"Our men lust after women not because of their breasts but because they are women. No man may marry a woman of the same tribe. In this way, the Seven Tribes are drawn together into one family."

Corvus continues, "For six summer passings, my people were happy and prospered. Then my mate died while giving birth to our child, who died at the same time. Because my people had forgotten they had ever lived, they had also forgotten people died. When my wife and newborn child died, no one knew what to do. The High Priest thought I was evil and thought I might cause much trouble because I was alone, and being alone, I would desire another mate, but there was no woman for my mate. He thought there would be no limit to my desire for a mate, and I would do many bad things. The High Priest would not listen to me. I was afraid I would be caged, like the sad-looking animals, so I left. The High Priest chased after me and tried to kill me, but I escaped across a great river.

"After three cycles of the smaller moon, I remembered the truth of coming here on a shaft of starlight, and that the God my people worship is a false god. If I return to my people and tell them the truth, I'll be killed. So I live without a people or a god."

After a lengthy pause, Butterfly says, "No one can live without a people or a god, but I do not know if my people or our gods will accept you. Is there no way your people will welcome you back?"

"I don't know. Perhaps if I had some great gift to give them. But I'm not sure I want to return."

Butterfly says, "The only gift I have to give is my knowledge, but compared to someone who travels on starlight between worlds, I must appear as a child."

"The medicine that you gave me to cure my sickness, we have nothing like it. I could take that back, but even that may not be enough."

"Lay back, close your eyes, and think of nothing."

When Corvus relaxes, Butterfly places a hand on either side of his head. He feels her presence within his mind and sees images of a particular white flower, moss, tree sap, tree bark, melons, nettles, mushrooms, and a dark green pod that grows on a vine. He sees the ingredients chopped, mashed, stirred together and cooked, and made into the two medicines Butterfly used to cure his illness.

When Butterfly finishes, she withdraws her presence, and a single tear slides down Corvus's right cheek.

"Crow, why do you cry?"

"The love I felt for my mate filled my heart. When she died, I felt I could not live. But just now, the way you entered my mind, I experienced you in ways I never could with my mate. It was like I no longer knew where I ended and you began. And I was able to look into your mind and see how you were almost not permitted to live because of your blindness."

"Yes, I am Miree, the nobody. For reasons known only to Grandmother, she protected me and so I lived. Because of my blindness, I am incomplete and will never have a mate, so I am nobody. Without a mate, I have no place in the community unless I become as Grandmother is, a healer and seer. But since you arrived, Grandmother has changed. It's as if she knows some great secret, and she is overcome with sorrow for what must be and can do nothing to change it."

Corvus repeats the name Miree, over and over. "I like how the name Miree sounds, but I do not like what it means. You're definitely not nobody; you are some-body very special."

"I like the name you gave me, perhaps one day I shall give you a name which only I shall know."

"I'd like that. Tell me more about your people. What do you think happens to a person when they die?"

"After someone dies, we lay their body out for the largest moon's cycle to give the animals a chance to eat the flesh. The night before the bones are gathered, Grandmother chews the leaves and journeys without moving to the council of gods, where she learns the will of the gods. If the gods say the person's spirit is good, the skull is taken and put in a niche in the back of the overhang for an entire year, that their spirit might bless our people. If the gods say the person's spirit is bad, the skull is crushed and thrown into the river that it might be swept out to sea, so the evil spirit will never find its way back to our people. Grandmother, and maybe one day me, but for certain when Grandmother dies, the gods will call to her spirit, and it shall find its tree that it may continue to live. I can show you many such trees, and anyone who wishes can go to one of the trees and ask for its help because it is wrong to ask the gods for help. What kind of god would it be if it granted people's desires? People know so little; gods know so much. Gods make sure that what must happen happens. That is why I think Grandmother is sad. She knows what must happen, and it saddens her heart, and she can do nothing but let it happen."

• • •

The next morning, Butterfly says, "I have thought much about all you have told me and have talked with Grandmother. I do not know how, after all, you've told me, you cannot be a god, yet why would you tell me you are not a god if it was not so? As a god, you would be loved and respected and welcomed into our tribe. But if you are not a god, then you must be a demon and must die. But I cannot believe you are a demon. I find only kindness, gratitude, and great sadness in your heart. Tonight, you must run away. Otherwise, tomorrow when you come before the people, I cannot protect you, and sadness will tear my heart to see you die."

Corvus says, "Sadness in my heart grows from the fact that I, like Darkness, despair of being alone. I fear being alone more than I fear death."

Suddenly, many angry voices are screaming. Butterfly listens, then says, "No! It is too soon!"

"What happened? What's too soon?"

"The elders say since you arrive hunting is poor, rain stops, and the biting flies swarm. They blame you. So, instead of waiting the one more day to make you well, Grandmother made the magic bloom die now. The elders call Grandmother many awful names. If you cannot make the magic bloom, then you, me, and Grandmother will die."

"Help me stand."

It's the first time in the three days that Corvus has put weight on his legs. They buckle.

Butterfly stops his fall. "You are still weak. You shouldn't be up."

Corvus grimaces, and pushing off her shoulder, manages to stand. Her shoulder is only chest-high.

"Where's the thing I carry on my back?"

Butterfly scampers away and returns a moment later.

Corvus puts weight on Butterfly's shoulder as she guides him out of the tall, nearly circular chamber ten feet in diameter and down a passage in which he must slightly twist to avoid scraping the walls. They enter a sandstone overhang three hundred feet long, fifty feet deep, and, near the front, thirty to forty feet in height. As his eyes adjust from the healing place's total darkness, he sees the morning twilight fading before the rising sun. A half dozen voices break into angry shouts at Corvus's approach.

For the first time, Corvus sees his hosts. The biggest males are four inches shorter than he is, but he guesses they are thirty pounds of solid muscle heavier. The women are a few inches shorter than the males. All are covered in fur which ranges in color from silver to rusty brown and light orange. The only clothing anyone wears is a bark loincloth. He looks down at Butterfly and sees that her fur varies from blood red to vibrant orange with a black lightning bolt between her breasts.

One woman who Corvus decides must be Grandmother steps between the men and Corvus, then shouts an odd assortment of guttural clicks and growls that he cannot envision ever making but remembers hearing when Butterfly found him. Sounds that he mistook for the growls of some beast about to prey upon him.

"I am sorry I brought you here. Only lightning or a god can make the magic bloom, and you say you are not a god, and I believe you."

"Lead me to where the magic bloom dances."

"My people do not understand god-talk. You tell me the words, and I speak for you."

In the center of the overhang, a third of the way back from the opening, is a ring of rocks three feet in diameter, lined with clay that is fire-reddened and hard as stone.

Corvus kneels beside the fire pit and removes his fire drill, which comprises two sticks, a length of cord, and a small rock, and sets them aside.

"If the elders think you trick them, your death will be made worse. You must make the magic bloom, like a god."

Corvus bites his upper lip. *What does Butterfly mean?*

*Make the magic bloom like a god?* He touches the ash with his hand; it's wet. Grandmother used water to put out the fire. He takes an arrow out of the quiver and spreads the foot-thick ash. Near the bottom are a few glowing red embers.

As Corvus replaces the arrow into his backpack, he whistles *The Ethereal Glade* and is pleasantly surprised to see people urgently whispering together.

"Never have my people heard such a sound come from anyone."

When Corvus is sure everyone has their eyes fixed upon him, he stops whistling, thrusts his left hand toward the Yellow Eye, and yells, "There!"

While everyone's attention is focused upward, Tobias reaches into his backpack's front pouch for a handful of tree bark strips, dry moss, pine needles, and leaves.

Then, bending low over the fire pit's center to block anyone from seeing, he drops the kindling.

A quick rush as men press into a tight circle.

Between chants of meaningless sounds and swirling hands, Corvus blows on the dying embers. After a few anxious moments, a tiny curl of smoke rises out of the ashes. Butterfly hands him several small twigs, which he arranges into a pyramidal-shaped lattice. After a few more gentle breaths, a tiny flame appears that he coaxes larger by adding ever-larger twigs until he has made the magic bloom with only his breath.

The crowd bursts into loud chattering.

Butterfly tells Corvus, "Grandmother tells the men you made the magic bloom as only a god can, and earned the right to live. The headman and others are not convinced. They say you must prove yourself in another test. You must also show courage and power over life."

Corvus meets the headman's eyes. "What must I do?"

Butterfly translates. "In four days, the two moons rise together full. All the Seven Tribes will assemble here, and a council of jaguars will gather. If you are a god, the jaguars will know, and you shall live; if you are a demon, the jaguars will know, and they will kill you and feast upon your carcass. They say that because I brought you to our home, if you run away, I shall take your place."

Corvus asks Butterfly, "Do you think I will run away?"

"You are either a god or a good man, and neither will run away. But I warn you; there is nothing worse than killing a jaguar. Killing a sacred jaguar brings disaster upon all the Seven Tribes. I have never seen the death to appease the gods, but I have heard it takes many days. You are cut in many places, and certain medicines are rubbed in the wounds to cause terrible pain. You are stung by many scorpions, whipped with thorns, suspended over the magic bloom like a wild boar, and many other things. Unless you can survive the jaguars without killing, you are doomed."

"You say you can talk to all creatures. Can't you talk to the jaguars and explain?"

"What would you have me do? Beg and plead for your life?"

Corvus shakes his head. "No. You saved my life.

Now, if I must give mine to save yours, I will."

"Just as you have gained Grandmother and my trust, you must convince the jaguars to trust you. Four days is not long, but perhaps something will come of our time together."

• • •

The following morning, all signs of sickness gone, Corvus wakes hungry. Patting the ground in a wide arc, he crawls, trying to find with his hands what his eyes cannot see. He stops at the sound of Butterfly's voice. "Crow, what are you doing?"

"I'm hungry. I'm looking for my backpack."

"Do not worry. I bring you food."

Butterfly appears beside him, holding a wooden bowl. "Our food is too poor for a god, so for the last three days, many people gather the lanilani, the food of gods."

Corvus dips his fingers in the bowl and immediately yanks them out. "It's moving. What is it?"

"*Lanilani* is the caterpillar of the silk butterfly. Only a god may eat. Everyone else who eats dies."

Corvus pushes the bowl away and says, "Others may think I am a god, but you know better. Where is the thing I was wearing when you found me?"

Butterfly scrambles away and returns with his backpack. Corvus takes out two honey-nut sticks, which comprise an inner white starchy tube from the center of a piece of cane that he rolls in honey and covers in nuts and seeds. He gives one to Butterfly and says, "This is what I eat."

"Then, I must not eat. I cannot eat the food of a god."

"But you know I am no god."

"I do not know what I know. But if you tell me to eat this, that I will not die, then I will eat." Corvus hears Butterfly smack her lips together. "It is good, so many things in one place. Maybe you could add mealworms and maggots; then, it would be delicious."

After they eat, Corvus walks with Butterfly to the edge of the overhang. When he made the magic bloom and saved Grandmother, he was too far from the edge, and it was too dark to see more than the vague outline of trees. But now, in full daylight, he discovers the overhang to be fifty feet above a circular clearing four hundred feet in diameter. The clearing is surrounded by trees taller than the Red Tower, with branches that entangle to form a canopy on which a monkey could travel for miles without ever coming to the ground. Beneath the trees is a thick undergrowth of vines, bushes, and shrubs. Vibrant flowers grow attached to the sides of trees, and in the rich decay of fallen trees are fungi of every color imaginable. But even more remarkable for someone who knows how to listen—the jungle is alive with chirps, squeaks, growls, the chattering of hundreds of different species of unseen animals.

Butterfly says, "We live inside the rock where nothing grows, and the magic bloom dies unless constantly fed. When we leave the rock, we descend into the world of the gods. Everything we need to live is there. We depend on the gods to live, so we must go carefully. We may not dig deeper into the ground than the roots of plants that are not trees, for that is where our ancestors' spirits live and nourish the world. That is why, whenever we leave the rock, we touch the center of the forehead, the upper world where the voices inside our heads dwell; then we touch the heart, the gods' dwelling place, and then clasp hands together and bow to acknowledge the ancestors."

Corvus does as Butterfly describes. *No one in Salem would acknowledge the world in such a way.* "Should I go first to guide your way?"

Butterfly laughs. "I have scampered up and down these cliffs since the day I was born. If I could not, I would not, even with Grandmother's help, have been permitted to live."

Corvus stops and cocks his head like a crow, trying to understand Butterfly's change in countenance as her body relaxes as she steps into the sunlight at the front of the overhang. After performing the ritual of leaving, Butterfly strolls onto a narrow ledge, leading a third of the way down to a series of footholds pecked into the bedrock. Corvus stands entranced, as Butterfly moves with a fluidity of motion he hasn't seen before. Far faster than he can believe, she is standing on the ground, smiling up at him.

"Aren't you coming?"

The footholds are spaced for the size of Butterfly's people, not for someone as tall as him, making Corvus's descent slow and difficult. When at last he stands beside

Butterfly, she says, "I thought you would fly down."

When he doesn't respond, she laughs.

Corvus can't decide if she is serious or mocking, but just as quickly decides it doesn't matter.

Butterfly says, "Stay close, or you will get lost. In our land, there are no paths, for it is said no way is easier or contains less danger than another. In this way, we learn every tree and rock the way a baby learns the contour of its mother's face. Is this not what your God teaches?"

"No, the God of my people teaches that the land was made for us to use," Corvus speaks with anger rising in his voice resulting from one of Erik's memories. "In the world I left to come to this world, we sickened the water and the air until the land nearly died."

Corvus feels Butterfly's hand on the side of his head. "Show me."

Corvus brushes her hands away. "No. You must not see, or you will hate me."

"I could never hate you. Did your people bring these old ways to my world?"

"No. We live much simpler. A day's walk in any direction and you wouldn't know we are there."

"My people have lived here beyond counting, and yet past the clearing, you would not know we are here. Maybe one day, you teach your people what mine already know."

As Corvus watches, Butterfly disappears in every way but physically into her surroundings. He realizes how little he knows her and how much like a child he must seem to her.

Butterfly takes Corvus's hand. "Three days. We must hurry slow, hurry so nothing is missed or left undone, slow so you can experience heart deep and learn a lifetime in three days."

Corvus often has to run to keep up with Butterfly, who flits through trees, marshy areas, and across streams as effortlessly as her namesake. She stops beside a tree with a red trunk, more massive in circumference than the fallen tree in the Ethereal Glade. Its smooth bark swirls upward like a corkscrew. There are no branches for over fifty feet.

"This is a wisdom tree. It is the largest tree in all the world and contains the spirits of the first two people created when Magic Bloom and Darkness lay together. Grandmother often comes here to seek wisdom."

"How do you talk to the wisdom tree? Will it tell me what I need to learn to survive the jaguars?"

"Crow, you are so angry at the God of your people, who you no longer love because He took your mate, that you have closed off your heart. Gods surround you, yet you neither see nor feel their presence. You see endless days alone because you look too far. Instead of ten summers or one summer, look no farther than how long a sound from your music stick hangs in the air.

"Sit so that you can lean back against the tree. Close your eyes, so you are as blind as I. Say nothing, and listen first with your feet, then your legs, your belly, your arms, your chest. Listen until your body is so heavy it disappears into the ground. Relax, and you will feel without weight. Let what you receive flow out, so you are endlessly receiving and giving until you no longer can tell where you begin and all else ends. This is called the Circle of Always Becoming. When you have entered the circle, all the wisdom of the trees, the ancestors, and the gods will flow into you."

Corvus closes his eyes, breathes deep, and grimaces. He had felt something like what Butterfly describes during his second visit to the Ethereal Glade, when he felt like he was sinking into the fallen log. It ended badly. But, Corvus thinks, *I am not there. I am in a strange land with someone who belongs to the world in a way I never will.*

As he relaxes, trying to understand what it means to listen with his feet, he sees the surrounding forest within his mind's eye and thinks he has achieved something good. He holds that picture while he listens and imagines each sound as a particular bird, monkey, or croaking frog.

"No! You are listening with your mind. That will make you a great hunter, nothing more."

That night, Corvus sees Butterfly talking to an adolescent man. From a distance, even without needing to hear what's said, which would only be a confusing garble of sounds anyways, he can tell they are fighting. Each is saying something hurtful to the other.

When Butterfly comes to him, Corvus says, "The young man is jealous."

"Taj-jul and I grew up together. He always felt sorry for me. When no one else would play with me or talk with me, he was there. Last year, after it was announced he would marry a girl of the Falcon people, he said we should run away and live as a couple. I said no; it's not permitted that two of the Jaguar people should marry, so I call him stupid and many bad names. But now that the one he is to marry has bled for the first time, he becomes more insistent."

Corvus says, "Taj-jul loves you."

"Is that the kind of love you are the god of?"

"No, that love is always hungry. The love I speak of is when one person's spirit and the spirit of another person lay with one another. Their offspring is a love that continues after death."

"Is that the love you shared with your mate that died?"

"Before I learned my God was no God, I would have said yes. Now I do not know what I know."

"At last, I understand. Come, let's go to the healing place."

Corvus says, "I don't understand."

Butterfly laughs. "Of course not. You are a man, and maybe a little god, but mostly a man."

Butterfly and Corvus lay upon their sides, only inches apart. Butterfly lightly touches every inch of his face and then kisses his forehead, nose, and lips. Corvus spasms back, then moves in and returns the kiss.

Butterfly, trying to remove his second skin, grunts in frustration.

Corvus puts a finger across her lips, then removes his shirt and pants as Butterfly removes her bark loincloth. They linger over and touch and kiss every part of the other's body. In the absolute darkness of the healing place, Corvus feels Butterfly enter his mind. Not the way she did when teaching him the cure, but like Magic Bloom merging with the Darkness, each losing themselves within the other. Within his mind, Corvus sees Butterfly not as how he remembers her face or body, the softness of her fur or her laughing purr, but as a beautiful golden-green light that flows, moves, and swirls. He sees himself as something dark blue, almost black, that struggles to move, like he's mired in mud. As he enters Butterfly and they each gasp in pleasure, he sees himself transformed into a golden-green light, no longer distinguishable from Butterfly.

Afterward, Butterfly snuggles against him and whispers, "You have learned to see with more than your eyes."

· · ·

When Corvus wakes, he reaches for Butterfly. *She's gone. She's talking to Grandmother.* He rolls onto his back. *Of everything that happened last night, the physical pleasure of our coming together is the least important and feels as distant and unimportant as Erik's Earth. What matters most is Butterfly coming to me in her purest form, a golden green light, and just as she cured my physical body of a deadly illness, last night she gave me the first dose of medicine to heal my spirit, something Miriam could never do.*

*Last night Butterfly said I have learned to see with more than my eyes. When Butterfly says listen first with your legs, the listening she means isn't about sounds, words, or music. Just as eyes are but one way of seeing, ears are only one way of listening. After all, sound isn't real until the waves of air on which it glides enter a mind...*

A clear, calming voice, Butterfly's voice, "You stand in your way. You see yourself as something apart, when the only difference between you, me, the gods, the ancestors, and nature is how well you listen. With practice, you will learn not to be afraid. You will learn that all that is, was and ever will be is too much to be contained within the space created by Darkness, but fits easily within a single tear cried by Magic Bloom."

In the healing place's total darkness, Butterfly reaches down, and Corvus instinctively reaches up and grasps her hand. He is surprised how easily she pulls him to his feet.

"Last night..."

Butterfly puts a finger across his lip, "Do not weaken what happened with words. Grandmother says I must take you to the Hollow Rock. Before I was afraid, but now I'm not, and neither should you be."

Just as the sky has lightened enough to hide the brightest star, Corvus and Butterfly stand in the clearing center in front of the Jaguar people's home.

Butterfly lets go of his hand. "Close your eyes and listen, then tell me what you see."

"It is like coming into a dark place after being in strong light. I cannot listen all at once, but I must let it happen gradually. As I listen, it's like my second skin falling away to reveal what lies beneath. And what lies beneath is— no! Like yesterday, I see trees and flowers, birds flying, and monkeys moving among tree branches."

"Do not let anger in. Anger, like a hungry jaguar,

isn't satisfied until it has killed and feasted. Remember, a baby doesn't learn to walk by walking. A baby learns to walk by falling. And each time they rise a little wiser."

Standing on her toes, Butterfly pulls Corvus down to her, kisses his lips, and whispers, "We have far to go and much to do before nightfall."

For the first two hours, Butterfly moves with the swiftness and confidence of someone who knows every rock and tree, then stops. "Grandmother says I must not take you farther. I must let you find your path to the Hollow Rock. It is a place special to all the Seven Tribes. It is where boys come to become men, and the ancestors' spirits gather to sing, dance, and perform rituals to help my people in the time of need."

"But how…"

Butterfly places a finger across his lips. "Listen. Remember, no path is shorter or less dangerous. Once there, you must three times strike the rock with the wooden club which only the strongest of my people can lift, then sit in the center of the rock and chew these leaves."

Butterfly hands Corvus a half-dozen small, fresh leaves that smell of lemon and mint.

"When I arrive, should I enter the Circle of Always Becoming before I chew the leaves?"

"No, the spirits of the ancestors are too strong. They would enter you and overwhelm you and make you crazy. Chew the leaves and play my music stick. It is made of a branch broken off of a fallen wisdom tree. You may not find the answer you seek, but you will find what you need."

Corvus takes Butterfly's flute and wonders how she carried it, since he hadn't seen it before. "Where will you be?"

"I will be close, awaiting your return."

"Return from where?"

"Crow, do not worry. If things go badly, I will know, and I will fight to bring you safely back. You must trust me as I trusted you when you told me I would not die if I ate your food."

"What should I play? I don't know any of your sacred songs."

"Chew the leaves, then play your heart. Now close your eyes and listen."

When he opens his eyes a moment later, Butterfly has vanished.

*A hollow rock sounds like something from a dream. Maybe what Butterfly means is a cave. Cave or not, my only hope of finding it is to listen.*

Closing his eyes, Corvus lets his mind fill with the sounds of the forest, and in his mind, sees the source of the sounds.

"No! You are listening with your mind!"

Corvus takes a deep, relaxing breath, and remembers this morning as he stood in the clearing, and how this morning he failed to see. *A baby doesn't learn to walk by walking but by falling, each time rising a little wiser.*

"No matter how long you wait to start, you will never be prepared."

Corvus grunts then bulls his way two dozen steps forward. When he looks back, he can't tell where he started. The tree's thick canopy and a layer of low clouds block any trace of sun and sense of direction. Like in the Tangled Hills, the only directions he can know are up-stream and downstream.

Listening isn't about sounds, it's about awareness.

Corvus starts walking, relaxing his mind, letting objects blend into one another until his body, moving independently of conscious input, flits like a butter-fly through the tangle of undergrowth and deadwood. How far he walks, how many corners he turns, or how many times he backtracks on himself—all blur into a single moment.

Dropping to his knees, Corvus cocks his head and traces with a finger the outlines of geometric figures, stick-figure people, and animals pecked into a low black basalt cliff.

Moving trance-like, Corvus climbs to the top of the rock outcrop and finds, as he knew he would, a four foot long wooden club. Lifting the small end, Corvus pulls at the club to judge its weight. With luck, he might lift it, but to strike the rock with any force? Corvus takes a deep calming breath, closes his eyes, reaches out for Butterfly, but she's gone.

*No, Butterfly has not abandoned me. She is nearby, but I am beyond her help.*

Corvus tightens his grip around the club handle, closes his eyes, takes a deep breath. *My mind must not get in my way!*

In a single fluid motion, Corvus raises the club above his head and lets the club's weight do the rest. The rock reverberates with a deep, hollow sound. After striking the rock for the third time, he drops the club, sits in its center, and chews the leaves Butterfly gave him.

Long after the sound has faded to silence, Corvus feels the rock continue to vibrate.

Taking up Butterfly's flute, he is amazed at its deep rich sound. Realizing he has no control over either the notes or the rhythms he plays, Corvus lets himself disappear into the music.

*What's happening? How am I inside the rock? What is the source of the light?*

A few feet in front of Corvus stands a man with no hair upon his head or face, half again taller than he is. The man is bent forward, fists touching the ground. His arms, legs, and chest are massive, muscular, and covered in thick black hair.

Corvus yells, "Who are you?"

The man bares his teeth and roars, then drops onto his knuckles and charges, passing through Corvus like neither are real.

Corvus runs after the brutish man down a narrow passage descending ever-deeper into the earth. The deeper he descends, the tighter the passageway, the lower its ceiling, and the darker and colder it becomes. When he can no longer see the man, Corvus stops and gasps for air.

*Who is this brutish man, and why must I follow him?*

As his breathing and heart rate return to normal, Corvus rubs his cold arms and whispers, "If I leave, nothing's changed, nothing's happened, and I will have failed not only myself but also Butterfly."

Corvus rolls his shoulders, clenches and unclenches his fist, arches his back, then strides forward. The passageway continues to narrow and grow lower, forcing Corvus onto his hands and knees, then onto his belly. Soon there is only darkness and cold, the rough basalt rock scraping his hands and tearing his clothes, and only one direction—forward.

When Corvus reaches out to pull himself forward and grasps nothing but air, he instinctively scoots back from the edge and bites his upper lip. *In the Canyon Ordeal, when I could go no farther, I found a way.* He pulls himself forward so he can fully extend his arm straight out and down. Nothing. *At the time, it seemed certain death to dive into the river.*

Corvus scrunches forward, past his waist, his legs rising to the top of the passageway. When his feet are no longer able to hold him, he falls.

The longer and faster he falls, the calmer Corvus becomes. As the rocks glow with a greenish-yellow light, he hears music. It is the very music he is playing outside, sitting on top of the rock.

As darkness rushes upwards, Corvus vanishes into a vibrant, red, sticky liquid that coats him. He claws his way out. Immediately the blood hardens, and he cannot move. He is in an enormous chamber that smells of lemon-scented honey. The brutish man is waiting.

The next moment, Corvus is tied to a long pole and suspended over a fire. The brutish man is turning the spit. Surrounding him are hundreds, maybe thousands, of Butterfly's people, but they are much smaller and all are able to fly with no need of wings.

*These must be the ancestor spirits of Butterfly's people.*

He wants to talk, but he can't move his mouth.

The ancestor spirits sing, and as they sing, the top of the cave opens, revealing trees, shrubs, flowers, birds, and all manners of beasts, but also something more—wisps of mist that swirl around, above, and through all things.

*These are the gods Butterfly sees everywhere.*

As he watches the gods, Corvus doesn't notice the blood burning away as he rotates above the magic bloom. When the last of the blood is gone, Corvus is on top of the Hollow Rock, holding Butterfly's music stick, and she is sitting beside him. He starts to speak, but Butterfly silences him with a finger across his lips, then pulls off the top of his second skin.

Here they spend the night.

• • •

The next day, as the sun's first rays clear the Flattop Mountains, Butterfly tells Corvus, "I must go and reach out to all jaguars and invite them to the gathering of tribes. You come as well and introduce yourself. Let them see you are not afraid."

As Butterfly navigates the forest, she is no longer playful or chatty. Whenever Corvus speaks or tries to reach out to her with his thoughts, it's like an impenetrable bubble surrounds her. And with every passing moment, the forest closes in and the air becomes denser and something else. It isn't until hours later, when But-terfly stops in a small clearing that opens onto a patch of sky, that Corvus realizes what that something else is—the forest isn't just quiet, it's without sound.

When Butterfly stops, she repeats the ritual of leav-ing the overhang, then collapses into a sitting position with her legs crossed. She whispers, "Remember what you felt at the Hollow Rock. Do not get lost inside your head. Sink, as into water, and you will come out the other side where the gods wait."

Corvus sits beside her, immersing himself in every sound as if he's outstretched in the Doorway's warm, spring-fed pool. As he listens, Corvus fills himself to overflowing with emptiness. He breathes in life without form or substance. His body dissolves and merges with the golden-green light he first saw in the Ethereal Glade, then later when he first lay with Butterfly. *Gods, people, plants, and animals are meaningless distinctions.*

Hours that seem like seconds later, Corvus feels a tap on his arm as gentle as the butterfly that awoke him from his vision during his second visit to the Ethereal Glade. His eyes flutter open upon an image of Butterfly smiling.

"With practice, you'll find it easy to enter the Circle of Always Becoming. Perhaps one day, you will achieve what few ever do: live forever within the Circle."

"Are you able to live within the Circle?"

"No, I get too distracted by all that happens within my community. I think only someone who lives alone or with but one can achieve this goal. Let's go home."

"Home? Do I have a home with you?"

"At the gathering of the tribes, it's announced when two people commit to a union. If you will have Miree, the Nobody, I will have Grandmother announce our intention."

"No, not Miree the Nobody, but Butterfly the Beautiful." After a thoughtful pause, Corvus asks, "Then you think I will live?"

"The Crow of three days ago had no chance, but... Tambour, the man who travels on starlight, has every chance. Do not let anybody know this name. Just as Butterfly is the name only you know, Tambour is the name which only I know."

By the time they return, the number of people at the overhang has swollen from the twenty-something of the Jaguar people to more than two hundred, and still they arrive.

"I will go first. I must talk to Grandmother alone."

Tambour stands on the crowd's edge and watches as the crowd parts, creating a path where none had existed for Butterfly to follow. Once she is inside the overhang, Tambour moves into the crowd. As he does, everyone goes quiet, grudgingly steps aside, and glares. As soon as he passes, the crowd closes ranks and explodes with laughter.

When finally he stands inside the overhang, Tambour sees Grandmother embracing Butterfly. When Butterfly turns to leave, Taj-jul is beside her. Butterfly nods and wipes a tear from his cheek, then guides Taj-jul to the healing place where he may cry unnoticed and gives him medicine which helps with sleep.

As Luna and Selene rise full, with Selene a slightly

darker circle within Luna's bright center, everyone except Grandmother leaves the clearing for the safety of the overhang. The headman smiles a toothy smile as he explains to Tambour what is about to happen.

*Butterfly is right. Three days ago, I had no chance.*

The headman thrusts the bow and arrows towards him. Tambour takes a step back, raises his arms, and shakes his head. The headman, stepping forward, emits a low-pitched growl that ends with a snarl and again pushes the bow and arrows in Tambour's hands.

Through clenched teeth, Tambour hisses, "Fine." He looks to Butterfly. *She's worried.*

After descending the cliff to where Grandmother waits, Tambour throws the bow and arrow as far as he can.

Not wanting the blood to soak into and permanently stain his clothes, Tambour removes his second skin. Grandmother nods and tips the wooden bowl filled with blood on top of his head and moves it back and forth, so it flows down both shoulders, chest, and back. The smell of fresh blood will attract any jaguar in the area and enrage its mind with lust for the kill.

Once she finishes her grisly task, Grandmother moves with surprising speed and grace and climbs to the ledge to stand beside Butterfly.

Tambour moves to the center of the clearing. The test is simple; survive. Breathing deeply, he spreads his arms wide, tips back his head, and smiles. As he reaches out with every cell in his body, Tambour feels himself spreading into each blade of grass and tree. He watches the progress of the jaguars through the eyes of birds, lizards, and small mammals. Even when the crowd gathered in the overhang gasps as they hear the growls of not one or two, but three jaguars, Tambour doesn't move.

The growls come closer and louder. Tambour sees himself as a golden-green light flowing into the jaguars, then just as suddenly the feeling disappears. The golden-green light is replaced by a blue, almost black, brute, unreasoning force. The crowd grows tense. They, too, no longer hear the jaguars, and they know of only one thing that might scare three jaguars.

Tambour, leaping for his bow, places an arrow between his teeth and another on the string. A wild boar—six feet high at the shoulder and nine feet long, with two sets of razor-sharp, outwardly turned tusks and a dark blue, nearly black hide covered with long, sparse, prickly hair—bursts into the clearing, charging straight for him.

The crowd shouts. Never were they expecting such a spectacle.

Tambour fires from a kneeling position. The arrow finds its mark in the boar's right shoulder, causing it to buckle slightly to that side as Tambour rolls away in the opposite direction.

The boar charges past.

Tambour jumps to his feet just as the boar turns to charge again. In one fluid motion, Tambour puts an arrow to the string and pulls it back. Without the benefit of aiming, the arrow enters the boar's left eye at a distance of fewer than five yards.

Immediately, the boar collapses onto its front knees and skids forward. Tambour jumps out of the way, but in a last instinctive move, the boar jerks its head to the right and grazes Tambour's right thigh with a tusk.

The crowd, not understanding how Tambour could kill a wild boar, roars its disbelief and approval. Even the headman jumps and shouts. Immediately, people swarm down the cliff and begin butchering the wild boar.

"Thanks to you, tonight my people will have a feast like no other."

Tambour feels a hand on his elbow and lets it guide him forward.

Butterfly, carrying his second skin, says, "We must get the blood out of your hair before it dries and the flies swarm, and we must quickly cover your thigh where you bleed. In the excitement and you soaked in blood, nobody noticed, but I notice."

Butterfly leads him to a nearby pool. "This place is where women go to clean when they bleed between times of babies."

After washing and dressing, Tambour and Butterfly start toward the overhang. In each of the six great fires lit from the one Corvus had restored, a large section of wild boar is cooking.

Tambour asks, "What of the jaguar test?"

Butterfly shrugs, "What you have done tonight will be remembered by many children, past any alive now."

Tambour listens. He listens as someone who has learned how to listen; he hears the drums, long hollow tree trunks, and thin pieces of wood that thrum as they swing above their heads. "The music speaks not of joy but of tragedy and horror. Do you hear it, too?"

"Yes, and it frightens me. Maybe Grandmother understands."

As soon as they enter the overhang, the headman waves them over. After making a lengthy speech, the headman holds up the wild boar's heart.

Butterfly says, "You must eat the heart to gain the wild boar's strength and courage."

As Tambour looks at the raw, bloody heart, his shoulders droop and his face goes white.

"Tambour, what's wrong?"

"Just before my mate died, I had a dream I was a vulture circling down from very high. I landed beside something freshly dead. I ripped at a bloody heart with my beak and feet, and when I looked, I saw I was eating my heart."

"That was a dream; this is not. Eat, or it will go bad."

Tambour grimaces as he licks his lips, then, taking the bloody heart, he raises it high for all to see before squashing it into his face and ripping out a chunk.

As he chews, he hears Butterfly say, "Offer it to the headman, and say the headman of each of the Seven Tribes are to share. Doing this will make you a great and benevolent god."

Tambour turns to the headman. "You and all the Seven Tribes' headmen must eat."

The headman looks puzzled until he hears Butterfly's voice, then his chest swells in size as he grows in stature. He rips out a chunk and, for a long moment, pauses as he looks between Tambour, Butterfly, and Grandmother. He growls and passes it to a headman of another tribe, who nearly rips it out of his hands. As the heart is passed, each headman pushes and shoves aside the others as they seek to be next,

After dinner, the upcoming unions are announced. When Grandmother announces Butterfly and Tambour's intention to form a union, she uses the names Miree and Keltai Lani, which Butterfly translates as 'the god who holds all in his heart.' Grandmother waits for any objection but hears none as Taj-jul, the only one who might, lies asleep in the healing place.

After the announcements finish, one elder after another from every tribe tells stories that Butterfly translates for Keltai Lani. One tells the origin story which Butterfly had told him; another tells how Magic Bloom got her name. Others tell stories of great battles with evil spirits, and so on until the central fire burns low and young children are led away by their mothers.

When only the men remain, Keltai Lani is brought to the center of the circle, in which no woman may sit.

Butterfly whispers to his mind, *"The headman wants you to show how you killed the wild boar."*

Keltai Lani groans. At the wrecked cargo ship, Tobias and Erik had discussed the dangers of giving people something they never knew existed and didn't need to thrive and had concluded it was a bad idea.

Keltai Lani holds the bow and arrows high and looks into the anxious faces of the tribal elders. "When you ask how I killed the wild boar, you ask the wrong question. The question you should ask is: why have I come here? Why do I appear as I do? I am Keltai Lani, the god who holds all in his heart. I am Keltai Lani, the forgotten, who can see into the hearts of the Seven Tribes' men." Rattling the bow in one hand and shaking the quiver in the other, he continues, "You have seen how these can kill a wild boar and think how easy it will make hunting, which is true, but what can kill animals can also kill people. This, I cannot allow. Until I know it will kill only for food, no one shall know its secret."

Keltai Lani tosses the arrows onto the fire, then, planting one end of the bow on the ground, steps in the center and bends the top end toward him until it breaks before tossing it too onto the fire.

There is a gasp. Some try to rush forward, while others hold them back. A moment of uncertainty ends when the oil Corvus rubbed into the bow and arrows to keep them pliant flares in a bright blue flame. When that happens, silence spreads across the men as they mourn their loss, followed by a steady increase in shouting and fist waving.

As if neither seeing nor hearing, Keltai Lani squats, and with one finger draws pictures in the sand blown into the overhang over the centuries. The men grow quiet as they press in tight to see what he is drawing.

Butterfly whispers. "The men think you are making powerful magic with the pictures you draw."

Keltai Lani brushes his hand across the sand, erasing the lines, then stands. "Tonight, I listened to the stories you tell of the gods and the time before remembering. All know the songs, dances, and rituals to appease the gods, but how many know how to see by listening?

How many among you don't just believe in the gods, but see the gods surrounding you? I appear to you as I am to teach the Seven Tribes that the gods are like strangers to you. I came sick and near to death, looking for compassion. I found it in only one: the one called Miree, the nobody, the incomplete. Tonight, Grandmother proclaimed our intent to union. Tomorrow we leave, never to return."

Butterfly prompts Keltai Lani, "Look into the magic bloom. Tell what you see."

As he stares into the fire, Keltai Lani whistles the tune he played when he sat upon the Hollow Rock. When he finishes, his voice changes tone and texture. "I see where we are growing dark and quiet—the clearing below withered and dead. Women and children wail for husbands and fathers. The Seven Tribes reduced to a single spark. Whether the spark goes out is not for me to say. The fate of the Seven Tribes is theirs to choose. In one cycle of the larger moon, as the sun sets upon the longest day, at the gathering of the waters where Darkness and Magic Bloom first lay in perfect union, a flower shall float upstream. If the Seven Tribes have this night learned the teaching of Keltai Lani, the flower shall open when the moon is at its highest. If the flower remains closed, the Seven Tribes shall fade as stars before the sun."

*What am I saying?*

"You are speaking with the Circle's voice."

"Now, I leave the circle of men. Tomorrow, Miree and I leave the world of men. Let any bad thoughts or feelings that have arisen among the Seven Tribes because I have come into your presence burn to ash like wood in the magic bloom."

"Say no more. Walk quickly to the healing place."

The men open the circle to form a path where none had existed.

Butterfly quickly joins him.

Tambour asks, "What happens now?"

"We wait."

"I don't know what came over me. When you told me to look into the magic bloom and tell what I saw, it was like someone else was talking."

"When you speak with the Circle of Always Becoming's voice, where do you end and the gods begin? As you spoke, I felt fear grow among the men, because they know you speak words of power. But being afraid makes men angry, and angry men often act foolishly."

Tambour feels a presence pass by. *Taj-jul?* Butterfly says, "Grandmother says women and children are leaving. She says the men are plotting to kill you. Even now, the men smoke and dance for courage. They know that in the healing place, you are trapped and cannot leave except through them. Grandmother says we must be ready. When the light explodes, we must be ready. But first, I must cover you in blackness so none may see or smell you."

No sooner has Tambour agreed than Butterfly disappears into a deep recess of the chamber and returns with a stone bowl. "We use black water to make our baskets hold water."

Tambour reaches into the bowl and scrapes out three fingers full of thick fluid. He holds it to his nose and says, "My people call this pitch."

He strips and crams his clothes into his backpack. Butterfly says, "You may not take this. It will make you slow when you need to be fast."

As the night goes on, Tambour grows uneasy as the cave empties of women and children and all the fires go out except the central one around which the dancing, drumming, and chanting rise to a frenetic rhythm.

"Grandmother says, 'look away, close your eyes.'"

The cave explodes with light.

Butterfly grabs Corvus's arm. "I see without eyes. I will lead."

Just as quickly as the light had exploded, it fades into blackness darker than the healing place, then slowly returns to the sun's brightness. Men howl and cry out in great pain, blindly striking out with their spears in all directions. Sometimes the spear finds its mark among friends and relatives. Others run off the ledge and fall to their deaths.

Butterfly runs, holding Tambour's arm, for the narrow path that leads to the footholds. When they reach the footholds, she says, "Hurry!"

For the first time, Tambour dares to open his eyes and look back. He stares at the mayhem and violence. Grandmother is among the dead and dying.

Taj-jul is fighting to keep the men from Butterfly. "I'm so sorry."

Butterfly says, "No time! Hurry!"

Out of carelessness bred from hurrying fast when he should hurry slow, Tambour misses a foothold and falls the final ten feet, spraining his ankle. Looking up, he sees Butterfly still on the ledge, covered in blood. She has been fighting to give him time to escape. A man races toward Butterfly. Taj-jul steps in front of Butterfly and takes the spear meant for her, and either he falls onto Butterfly or Butterfly reaches out to catch him, Tambour cannot tell, but the result is that together they fall. Tambour crawls over and flings Taj-jul's body aside. Blood oozes from Butterfly's mouth, her eyes unclouded and open. She forces a smile, then goes limp.

The effect of whatever Grandmother used to make the light explode has worn off. The men are coming to their senses and see the carnage they wrought while their minds were enraged. They look into the clearing and see Tambour, covered in black, lit by the two full moons nearing zenith.

Immediately, the men begin down the cliff. Tambour, hobbling upon his sprained ankle and carrying Butterfly's lifeless body, hurries into the forest. He stumbles and falls. His pursuers grow close.

"Leave me. I will guide you."

A minute later, he has crawled into the hollow side of a large fallen tree covered with moss.

"How can you speak?"

"My spirit has found its tree. Be strong. Be silent."

Tambour listens as his pursuers run by, unable to see or smell him because of the pitch.

Before dawn, men joined by women and children return to the scene of the slaughter. Listening to their inconsolable wails, the dam breaks on Tambour's feelings.

He cries until he becomes dry as the Great Emptiness.

"Tambour, a short distance away, the ground is hollow. I will guide you. The way in is a narrow slot hidden by a fallen tree. You must lie flat and scoot to enter. Stay there for three days, then leave and never return."

Tambour finds the cave and sighs. Condensation dripping from the roof has formed a small pool, but there is no food. It is not the first time he will go so long without food. *But what does it matter? Butterfly is dead, and I am alone.*

• • •

After three days, Tambour emerges from the hidden cave. The sky, covered by low clouds, is drizzling waves of warm rain. He returns to the clearing. Over forty men slaughtered because of his...*what? What had he done that was so bad? How can you know what you don't know?*

Tambour stops beside the body of Taj-jul, his belly, arms, and legs ripped open, a feast for carrion birds, scavengers, maggots, and worms of all sorts.

Tambour finds his backpack at the base of the overhang, its contents scattered and his flute broken. Gathering together his second-skin, Tambour goes to the pool in which Butterfly bathed him after the jaguar test and cleans himself of the dry pitch he hasn't already picked off.

Remembering what Butterfly said of the treatment of bodies after death, Tambour does not bother searching through the rows of neatly laid out bodies. Instead, he retraces his steps of that fateful night and nearly passes Butterfly's body without seeing. Tambour leans back and growls. Butterfly's body has been hacked into pieces and her skull crushed.

Her people may have judged her evil, but the gods knew better and let her spirit enter a tree.

Taking Butterfly's flute from just above her right breast, Tambour replaces it with his broken flute, then, following no path, walks among the giant trees. At last, he stops beside one and leans into it and says, "Before coming to the Pathless Forest, I talked to trees, but I never knew why. Now I talk to this tree because I know it's filled with Butterfly's—known to her people as Miree, who was anything but nobody—wisdom."

"Tambour, you must leave. But first, explain to me how I see living within you a man who fishes for and catches the sun. How can that be!? You are not strong but gentle, and gentleness, when not weakness, is good."

"That is the man I may one day become. Perhaps one day, when my spirit is no longer heavy with anger and grief, I shall remember how to enter the Circle of Always Becoming. Perhaps one day, I shall learn to listen and gain in wisdom, so when I die, my spirit will find its tree."

"That too is my wish for you. But first, you must forgive yourself. I died not because of anything you did. Grandmother knew what must happen. Even that first day, when you made the magic bloom as only a god could, Grandmother knew you were no god, but someone with a good heart. She knew that what you are is worth protecting, so she helped you. When I told her of our desire to form a union, she cried tears of joy. Now that I have found my tree, and all wisdom is made plain to me, I know that from the moment I found you, Grandmother knew what must happen. It made her sad, but she had the courage to say and do nothing but let what must happen happen."

"How long shall your spirit remain with this tree?"

"It shall remain as long as the tree lives."

"And when the tree dies?"

"Wisdom never dies or is lost. When the tree falls and decays into soil, my wisdom shall nourish the land, its plants, and creatures. Tonight, make your camp in the place I found you, and once more, play your flute. Tambour, I have learned so much from you, but the best I learned is what it means when two spirits unite and give birth to that which lasts beyond time."

That night, as the sun is setting, Tambour removes Butterfly's flute from his backpack, and as he watches the Pathless Forest disappear into darkness, he thinks. *If I was alone before, how much more alone am I now? And like everything else I've seen, done, and experienced since entering the Red River Canyon, all that we shared and all that I've learned from Butterfly must remain a secret. But why? Why must it remain a secret? The Final Day of Creation, when I saw and heard God speak, pales in comparison to the time I spent within the Circle of Always Becoming.*

*If I can teach Salem's people to see gods all around them, to feel the interconnection with all living things, they would thrive in ways not measured in people or livestock or storage bins over-flowing with surplus food. I could teach them what Butterfly's people already know—how to live so gently as to go unnoticed.*

Closing his eyes, Tambour strokes Butterfly's flute against his cheek. With tears sliding down his cheek, Tambour sighs into the flute and discovers that, like when he sat upon the Hollow Rock, he has no control over the notes or rhythm that he plays. When the last note sounds, Tambour speaks aloud, "This song I name *Paradise Lost* or *Tambour's Heartache.*"

After a moment of silence to allow the last reverberations of *Tambour's Heartache* to disperse, Tambour plays a single note and listens to see how long it hangs in the air, and discovers it endures the length of a single heartbeat. That, Butterfly said, is how far into the future one should live.

# CHAPTER FIVE

For the next three days, Corvus camps on the summit of the Flattop Mountains. Each day he replenishes his supplies, made difficult by the destruction of his bow and arrows, and each night he lights a bonfire large enough to be visible far beyond the home of the Jaguar people. *If only a god can make the magic bloom, then anyone who sees the fire will know that a mighty god lives here and that they must never come this far.* And each night, by the bonfire's light, Corvus writes an account of his time with Butterfly.

The third night after lighting the bonfire, Corvus plays *Tambour's Heartache*, then lets his shoulders sag and sighs. "I'm so..." he wants to use Erik's word—fucking—but it's not in his nature, "...tired of losing everyone I love. First Jenny, then Rebecca, and now Butterfly. What's the point of anything?"

"Oh, Tambour, have you learned nothing?"

"Butterfly?"

"You may leave the Jaguar people's homeland, but you can never leave the Pathless Forest. No matter where you travel, the Pathless Forest is where you live. Remember, you pass through the Pathless Forest by learning every rock and tree the way a baby explores its mother's face. Remember, no path is shorter or less dangerous.

"Yes, it's always dangerous to cross great rivers and places of great emptiness. The Jaguar people have special places to cross certain rivers, believing that because they follow in their ancestor's footsteps, the way is less dangerous. But what they tell themselves is a lie that gives them courage. Is that what you want? A lie to give you courage?

"You have spent three days preparing for what you cannot know. No matter how much you prepare, you will never be ready.

"If you think you are alone, that is because you have forgotten how to enter the Circle of Always Becoming. How can you be alone and a part of everything at the same time?"

In reply to Butterfly's last question, Tambour picks up her flute and plays all the tunes he's composed in the order that he wrote them as if by playing them, he is playing the story of his life. Just as the last note of *Tambour's Heartache* fades into silence a heartbeat later, he stares at his hands. *Tomorrow, when I leave, I leave Tambour, the man who travels upon starlight, the name only Butterfly knows, and only a man able to enter the Circle is worthy to claim, and descend into the world of Corvus, the unremarkable.*

Tambour bites his upper lip, the pain overwhelming his urge to act out his anger.

—7/26/8—

Ten days since leaving the Flattop Mountains, the last three without water or clouds and with temperatures that burn my feet through my shoes, I lie beneath a nearly dead tree growing on the edge of a cracked and peeling scab of ground that a month ago was a muddy pool. I see no purpose in going farther.

Butterfly, I have often worried about dying, alone and forgotten, that my death will go as unnoticed as the life I've led. But now that my death is upon me, I feel calm and peaceful. I would've liked to have found a way to share with my people everything you taught me. If I could get my people to see they live surrounded by gods and learn to enter the Circle of Always Becoming, they might fulfill what Lionel Rutger, for all the wrong reasons, could only dream: a people living forever in paradise.

Butterfly, if the gods look kindly upon my spirit, there's only this tree for my spirit to enter, which, like me, will soon be dead. And as there are no animals to eat my carcass, I shall become as shriveled and dried as the body of the wrecked cargo ship's pilot, Andrew. But instead of a cairn of stone, my memorial shall be a dune of sand.

Closing the journal, Corvus returns it into the backpack. Leaning back into the tree, he tries to play Butterfly's flute through dry, cracked, and swollen lips. His efforts go unsounded except for a pain-filled whimper.

*Three hours*, he thinks, *before the sun will set and the*

*sand starts to cool.*

Closing his eyes, Corvus remembers, *Atop the Red Tower, when I was as near to death, Rebecca and Naomi came to me and invited me to join them in a lush meadow. Then I was stopped because of crows, but here, there are no crows.*

Today, when Corvus reaches out, it's not for Rebecca or Naomi, but Butterfly. Touching his forehead to honor being alive. Touching his heart to honor the gods, the source of life. Then, clasping his hands, he bows to honor the spirits of—*who?* He has no ancestors on this world.

He thinks because he cannot speak, *Butterfly. Help me enter the Circle one last time.*

Butterfly laughs, "Tambour, you are only a man and maybe a little god, a very little god. It is not up to you to say when you die or what you can or cannot do. Remember, the gods do what they have to to make what must happen happen."

A prodigious clap of thunder marks the start of a half hour deluge of more rain than falls typically in three years.

Corvus silently whispers, "Thank you," then wonders which god or gods he's thanking.

While it rains, Corvus lays his water-skin flat and, like an animal, laps the water that gathers on top as the mudflat transforms into a shallow pool.

Two days later, strong enough to walk and with a full water-skin, Corvus watches sand dunes turn green with plants. Small amphibians emerge after a wait of months, perhaps years, for such rain. Without wasting a second or an ounce of energy, they engage in a frantic race to do what is necessary to ensure life will continue in a place life seems impossible.

• • •

Another ten days pass before Corvus, greeted by a gathering of crows screeching and squawking his safe return, sleeps on top of the overhang above his home by Floating Fire Lake, in which nothing can grow and where the magic bloom cannot live without being continuously fed. The next morning, he launches his canoe and paddles to the lake's center.

The lake is unblemished except for the rhythmic swell of passing ripples, which lulls him to sleep. He dreams that floating in the center of the lake is a flame, and out of the flame emerges a white water lily that opens its petals to reveal a soft greenish-golden glow that rises into the sky and becomes the sun.

When Corvus wakes, he thinks, *Before I left for the Pathless Forest, the flame opened like a flower to reveal a butterfly that vanished into a point of light that became life-giving rain. Now, the flame opens to reveal a greenish-gold sphere like I experienced when Butterfly and I merged. Then the orb becomes the sun, but not the black sun of my last visit to the Ethereal Glade, but a yellowish-green sun, the source of light and life. The sun, which the Sunfisher is arrogant and powerful enough to catch. The dreams are merging as if feeding off of each other.*

It is late afternoon before Corvus arrives at the lake's southern outlet. Before going on to *the Ethereal Glade,* he thinks how odd he never named the river he first followed to the lake or the river that emerges. "The river that enters from the north, I name Hope River because it was with hope that I came to this place. The river that enters from the west is the Calling River, but the river that leaves the lake deserves a name. If you begin with hope and add what is calling, what emerges? Destiny? From this time forward, I shall call the river of the Ethereal Glade the River Destiny."

After beaching the canoe, Corvus walks the short distance to the Ethereal Glade and once more stands atop the giant fallen log where he has twice encountered the Goddess. This time, he stands with the confidence that comes from surviving the jaguar test and crossing the Great Emptiness. Outstretching his arms and leaning back as far as possible, his upturned face is bathed in a yellow-green aura made of sunlight filtered through a dense canopy of leaves. Then, straightening, he takes Butterfly's flute, plays The Ethereal Glade, and is immersed in a warm, nourishing mist that tastes like lemon-flavored honey and makes him pleasantly light-headed.

Standing transfixed, Corvus watches a brown butterfly trimmed blue with cream-colored spots glide out of the mist and transform into the Goddess. She is wearing a long, thin white dress trimmed with a green border above a yellow border.

Corvus touches first his heart and then his forehead before clasping his hands and bowing slightly forward. "Goddess, the last time we spoke, you said I would find only questions without answers; instead, I found answers without questions, or so I thought. Since my last visit with you, I traveled far, suffered much, encountered the true inhabitants of this world, and learned of the Circle of Always Becoming. Within the Circle, there are no questions; there is only completeness. But now that I have lost my Butterfly and I am farther than ever from returning to Salem, my spirit is awash with questions without answer."

The Goddess' feet float just off the ground. Tilting her head side to side, she steps back with her left foot, then steps forward with her right and lifts it high. She pivots, making long strides that end in leaps and spins. She bends back so low her hair drags on the ground, then stops and extends an arm. "Tambour, dance with me."

"No. I am afraid if I do, I shall disappear into your embrace."

"Then tell me, where will you go and what shall you do?"

"At the heart of me stands the Sunfisher, and what he catches is the sun. Not the sun that glides overhead, but a golden-green orb, the source of life. Never did I ask what the Sunfisher will do with the sun once he catches it. The answer is, he will enter and become one with it. But before that is possible, I must learn to live within the Circle."

The Goddess dissolves into a golden-green orb. "Lie back on the log. Listen! What do you hear?"

As Corvus lies back, he feels himself sink into the log. "Crying? When Darkness heard crying, he was happy because he knew it meant he was not alone. But this crying is different. It's loud and heart-rendering as the crying following the frenzied slaughter of the Seven Tribes, but it's not about what has happened but what is happening. As if tears and wails of anguish unite to form a long snake, glowing orange."

"Go, they need you."

A cold cyclonic blast of wind answered by the sharp crack of a long-dead branch crashing a few feet away startles Corvus, breaking the spell.

Corvus shakes his head no and scoots back along the top of the log like he did the first night he spent in the Circle of Stones and backed away in terror from a vague, gray shape looming over him. "No, no one needs me. Certainly not the Seven Tribes. And the people of Salem? What do I have that they need? I destroyed one people with my coming. I won't do the same to another."

Corvus returns to the canoe and once again paddles out of sight of land. Just before dawn, he dreams he is standing on the highest mountain in all the world. Bubbling out of its summit comes pure, cold, sparkling water that divides into four great rivers. Each river is a distinct color: red, blue, yellow, green. He stands in front of each river, pulling the rivers forward as if each is a rope attached to an enormous weight. Before the red stands Sunfisher, before the yellow Corvus, before the green Tobias, and before the blue Erik. Each person, each river, has a unique path. As each river joins with the other, so do the different selves until there's but one river, the Red River, pulled by one self, the Sunfisher. As the Sunfisher approaches Salem, the people come down to the river, kneel upon its banks, and drink.

When Corvus wakes, he thinks, *Can the answer for once be so blatant? The four rivers are the Great Valley's lifeblood, united in me, and Salem's people are drinking what I have brought them. And what have I to bring them except a destroying truth of the Four Hundred's journey from Earth? Is that what they need, or should it, like all the useful crap in the cargo hold, stay with the cargo ship, and never enter into their lives? Who am I to make such decisions?*

"You are Tambour, the one who travels upon starlight."

"Butterfly, I'm not ready to return."

"No matter how long you prepare for what you cannot know, you will never be ready."

Corvus paddles to a spot on the eastern shore and begins walking.

In two days, he stands atop the Gateway Mountains, or, as he once called them and must again call them, the Forbidden Mountains, looking into the Great Valley.

Two days later, Corvus sits on the last hill's summit before the mountains give way to the Great Valley's rolling plains, watching twilight darken to allow the first stars to emerge. *What might my return to the Great Valley sound like when played upon Butterfly's flute?* He closes his eyes and listens as one who knows how to listen. *For is it not said the listening is the wisest of all the senses?*

He hears crying. After licking his lips and swallowing twice, Corvus slowly opens his eyes. Before him is a flickering string of orange lights, a glowing snake. *How,* he wonders, *can I hear crying from something so distant? If it is possible to speak out of the Circle, is it also possible to listen through it?* He pinches himself. What he sees is no dream. There, before him, is the snake made of crying, glowing orange.

Corvus watches until, just before sunrise, the snake stops and the fires go out.

# CHAPTER SIX

A few minutes past the sun's zenith, with the image of the glowing snake ever-present within his mind, Corvus slumps against a sprawling oak, his head tilted forward and his hands pressed hard against his ears. A short distance away is a scattering of twenty wagons, their sides extended upward and covered in thick, coarse cloth. No wagon is closer to another than twenty feet. No one is about. The only sounds are the snorts of horses at rest and the piercing screams of frightened children peppered with the unrestrained wails of adults.

A man coming out of a wagon stares at Corvus and yells, "Who are you? Who sent you?"

"Joshua, don't you know me?"

A female voice cries out, "Joshua! Go back to your wagon. You've plenty to do!"

Without a moment's hesitation, the man, barely glancing at the woman, disappears into the closest wagon.

"Now, who are... oh my God! Tobias? Is that you? You look a mess! No wonder Joshua didn't recognize you." The woman starts forward, then stops. "You chose a poor time to return. You'd best go back from wherever you came."

*Tobias?* Corvus chuckles silently. *Who else would I be*

*to the people of Salem?*

"Why? What's happening?"

The woman's face is pale, her eyes sunk to mere slits, her shoulders too heavy to lift, but her words are strong and precise, demanding attention and obedience. "Plague. At least half are dead. Soon we'll all be dead."

Tobias recognizes the woman as Miriam, whom Erik knew as Jenny.

"Maybe not. Not long ago, I was deathly ill, high fever, vomiting, eyes sensitive to light, and my skin easily burned. I spent several days in a dark place to avoid exposure to the sun."

Miriam nods. "Which is why we travel in darkness. Each night we leave behind our recent dead and stay inside during the day. But if you had what we have, you'd be dead."

"I might know a cure. At least let me try. Let me borrow a horse."

"Don't come close. I don't want your death on my conscience."

"Besides the horse, I'll need a half dozen good-sized containers, a mortar and pestle, two gallons of water, and two large cooking pots."

Miriam nods. "I didn't think you'd survive on your own, but you look fit and healthy," she laughs, "and rather unkempt, but that won't matter if your cure doesn't work."

"Asher, Gideon, Martha?"

"Dead."

Before Tobias can respond to the deaths of her mate

and two children, Miriam has walked away. Fifteen minutes later, she returns with a saddled horse and two bulging saddlebags. She stops fifty feet from Tobias and urges the horse forward. "I'll have someone leave the rest beneath the tree. I'd wish you good luck, but I don't think luck has anything to do with this. What we need is a miracle. Maybe God will listen to you. He doesn't seem to be listening to us."

*Why would He? God makes sure that what must happen happens. Maybe my return to the Great Valley at this time, like the boulder at the start of the canyon ordeal that was in the perfect place for me to jump onto, is more than a coincidence.*

Swinging himself onto the horse, Tobias urges it into a fast lope, pausing only long enough to wave. As soon as he is out of sight of the caravan, Tobias stops and leans into the horse's neck. The memory Butterfly imprinted in his mind of what to collect and how to prepare the ingredients is as clear as the programming done on the cargo ship to convince him he had seen and heard God. But knowing what to collect and finding it are two distinct things. Within his mind, he counts eight different ingredients.

"Oh, Butterfly, in the open grasslands of the Great Valley, I'll be lucky to find even two ingredients. I'd probably do better in the river valleys, but the Red River is most of a day's ride, and the Yellow River, while closer, is much smaller. It'll take days, maybe weeks, to find everything I need, and by then there won't be anyone to save."

In his mind's eye, Tobias remembers a hollow he

skirted on his way to the caravan protected on three sides by steep hills, warmed and nourished by a hot spring. When he first passed it by, Tobias called it an oasis of abundance, unlike anything he'd seen outside of the Ethereal Glade or the Pathless Forest, and had promised himself to one day return. He kicks the horse in the flanks. That one day is today.

Two hours later, Tobias hobbles the horse on the summit of one of the hills surrounding the hollow. After touching his heart, his forehead, and clasping his hands together, Tobias bows slightly forward. "Butterfly, I'm frightened that everything I collect will be wrong, and everyone will die."

"Tambour, you have come full circle. Death forced you apart from your people; now, death draws you back. Tambour, you are unique among all peoples, for you bear the fruit of two worlds you seek to keep apart, but must combine in you for your people to survive. Hurry slow, a few moments wasted now will save time and lives later. Close your eyes. Let beauty and love sweep fear and doubt aside."

Closing his eyes, Tobias floods his mind with a torrent of images: a mother deer with her fawn, a butterfly brushing the tip of his nose, crows playfully diving, the first time he lay with Butterfly, the Doorway's warm water, Rebecca's lavender scent.

"Listen well. Remember, you are not the cure; you are the path."

With the same confidence of being guided and supported he felt when climbing the moss-slick cliff out of the Red River Canyon and he felt when descending the Red Tower after his near-fatal fast, Tobias enters the protected hollow, fills the wooden jugs, and seals them tight.

After loading the containers into the saddlebags, Tobias scratches the horse's neck. "You, like me, were brought to this world. If the cure doesn't work and Salem's people are no more, I wonder, will you be as lost and confused as I when I realized I don't belong here, or will you wake to your wild nature and thrive?"

The horse, tossing his head and snorting, shakes Tobias back into the moment. "We must hurry. Every second is precious."

When Tobias arrives at the sprawling oak he named the Sorrow Tree, the sun is setting. Four men with shovels are climbing down from a wagon into which Tobias can't see, but guessing from the size of the grave they are digging, it contains ten or perhaps more newly dead.

With quick, sure movements, Tobias builds a fire. After filling each pot half full of water, he adds different combinations of the ingredients, continually stirring each until he has brought both mixtures to a boil. He has finished in a little more than an hour, but the pots and their contents are much too hot to touch. During the agonizing hours waiting for the pots to cool, Tobias watches the men fill in the grave and then ride after the caravan, snaking out in a long line, their paths lit by torches blazing beside each driver.

As soon as the pots are warm to the touch, Tobias loads the saddlebags and rides after the caravan. Miriam is driving the first wagon. When she sees Tobias riding up to her, she waves him away, "Close enough. Keep the horse. Leave the saddlebags on the ground. I'll come and get them." As she jumps down, she yells to the wagon driver behind her, "We'll go no farther," and mumbles under her breath, "What's the point?"

Tobias dismounts, drops the reins, and steps away from the horse.

Miriam looks at her fingernails, ragged from being chewed down to the quick, and asks without emotion, "What's the dose?"

"A small spoonful?"

Miriam looks up and laughs. "Very precise. How does it taste?"

"The yellowish paste not so good, the other very sweet."

"How long before it works? If it does."

"It'll take a few days for a complete recovery, but by morning there should be definite signs of improvement, plus it has the side-effect of making you sleepy."

Miriam twirls her hair around a finger. "If it doesn't work, at least it'll give the dying and their loved ones a glimmer of hope, even if it's for only a few hours. There's been a lot of gossip about why you returned. I worry that people might blame you if this doesn't work, so I suggest you leave until we know."

"I'll return to the tree where you saw me this morning."

Tobias leaves the horse, walks the two miles back to the Sorrow Tree, and leans against its trunk. He takes out Butterfly's flute and plays.

As soon as the morning sun clears the horizon, Tobias returns to the caravan. As he approaches, a man walking out to greet him rears back and hits Tobias on the jaw. Tobias allows himself to stagger and fall back onto the ground.

"I told Miriam it might not work."

"You shit-faced coward! That's just it! It does work! If you had arrived a day earlier, I wouldn't have buried my wife and last child."

"I'm sorry I didn't get here sooner, but how could I know…"

"Oh, I think you knew. I think you got crazy when your wife died and blamed us, and then, like the coward you are, ran away with your tail between your legs. I think somehow you sickened everyone and then showed up just in time to cure us, and now you think people will be so grateful we'll wait on you hand and foot. Well, I'm here to tell you it's not going to work. I'll see to that. I'll show people just what kind of bastard you are."

Miriam runs over and takes Daniel Tallgrass by the elbow and leads him away. "I apologize for Daniel, but he's not the only one who is angry the cure worked. Now that people are beginning to realize they're going to live, they need to figure out how to come to terms with what they've lost and the guilt for being alive."

"But Daniel is right. I could have easily arrived days earlier and…"

"Don't. What's happened has happened. I must remind everyone, myself included, to be grateful for what we have. And what we have is someone who can cure the plague. Right now, what I need from you are more ingredients. We need enough to treat the others."

"Others?"

"A week ago, we left Salem with everyone that showed no symptoms, except for the Priests and their families that stayed behind to bury the dead and the Elders and their families who stayed to turn out the livestock so they could fend for themselves and take in what harvest was ready. We had to do something to try to stop the plague. In such a small community, I doubt anyone wasn't already exposed. After they finish their jobs, the Priests and Elders will leave Salem and seek safety in solitude. The plan is that three weeks from now, any survivors will assemble in Salem."

"I know you're anxious to get the medicine to the others, but wait until I get back before you do anything. I'm not sure I can find any more of one ingredient."

A few minutes later, Tobias is riding off to the hot spring, but with a sinking heart. He already picked every one of the white flowers trimmed with pink—a key ingredient in both medicines—that he could find. But as he approaches the pool, his heart leaps out of his chest. The flower has more than replenished its numbers.

By noon, the medicine has been made. Riders are dispatched to find the Elders and Priests with the instructions to wait three days after beginning the treatment before returning to Salem.

As they watch the riders disappear, Miriam leans into Tobias and wraps her arms around him in a warm embrace and whispers, "Thank you."

"Jenny, you're welcome."

"Jenny? What an odd name. Why did you call me that?"

"Did I?"

"I don't understand. The recipe for the cure requires so many ingredients and is so complicated. How did you learn to make it?"

"Does it matter?"

"Where have you been for the last year?"

"Does it matter?"

"Yes, it matters. There will be people who will hail you as a hero, and some like Daniel will blame you for their loved ones' deaths. People will want to know where you've been and what you've done and how you knew to make the cure."

"Can't we just say that God inspired me to return with the knowledge to make the cure in your hour of need?"

Miriam takes a step back. "You've never lied to me."

Tobias smirks. Maybe he hasn't, but Erik often lied to Jenny and she always forgave him.

"What's so funny? And don't ask 'does it matter?' or I swear I'll punch you."

"Perhaps it's better for all that I leave."

"No. If we are going to survive, we need you, your strength, and what other secret knowledge you possess."

Tobias clenches his fists. "I'm not the same person that left Salem a year ago. If I stay, I might be as much a threat as the plague."

"That's impossible. Besides, I can't believe that the

man who fifteen minutes after returning and discovering the danger we were in leaves to find the cure is anything but kind and good. Undoubtedly, being away from Salem did change you, but from what I sense, if anything, it's for the better. I've got patients to check on. If you want, you can share my wagon; I've plenty of room."

Tobias shakes his head. "The crying is overwhelming."

"I know it sounds callous, but I no longer hear it. At first, like you, I was overwhelmed and could barely function, but I knew if I was to be of any good, I had to become immune. I know some people think I've become cold-hearted since I lost Asher and both children, but they don't know how much I suffer and how personally I feel each death."

"I know how personally you took it when Rebecca died, but that is nothing compared to this. Jenny, anybody who knows you knows you are a warm and caring person."

"That's the second time you called me Jenny. Who is she?"

Tobias takes a deep breath. He was never good at lying, but he can't tell Miriam the truth.

"After I crossed the Red River to escape Micah and the others, I entered a place I call the Tangled Hills, where, perhaps, I went mad, because after nearly being struck by lightning, I imagined, dreamed, hallucinated—I don't know what to call it—that before God created us on the Final Day of Creation, you, me, Rebecca,

Asher, everyone lived in another land, and in that land, you and I, not Rebecca and I, were lovers. You were called Jenny, and since seeing you again, I see you as Jenny and not as Miriam. Sometimes I have problems separating fantasy from reality."

"I wish this was a fantasy or a dream I could wake from instead of a nightmare I'm forced to live. Asher told me about your escape across the Red River. I never thought I'd see you again."

"When did the plague start?"

"Besides the riders that hunted you in the Great Valley, another group led by Silas went east through the gorge. The thinking was that it was the more likely route you'd take, since he didn't think you'd go anywhere near the quarry if you wanted to evade capture. Beyond the gorge, they found a place we now call the Land Bountiful. Five days' ride east from the gorge, the Red River empties into the sea.

"The search party returned after two weeks with the skins of fur-covered sea animals and goats with soft and beautiful hair, the horns of strange beasts, and sea creatures' shells. When they returned, people were so astonished all anyone could think about was having stuff they never knew existed but suddenly couldn't live without. Whenever not everyone was needed in the fields, hunting parties would go in search of even greater treasures. It became an absolute obsession. There was talk of building a new city there.

"You'd think Micah would stop it and remind people how we are all equal in God's sight and how material goods mean nothing when they are the source of jealousy and fighting. But he was among the worst of all. He decided that, as High Priest, he needed unique garments and decorations as badges of his office. And Silas agreed that his role as Chief Elder needed similar accouterments."

Miriam sighs as her shoulders droop. "The last hunting party returned a month ago. The plague struck two weeks later. So, I guess, in a way, if you hadn't run away, the Land Bountiful would never have been discovered, and the plague wouldn't have happened."

"Now wait, you can't blame me for other people's behavior."

"No, of course, I don't blame you. Although there might be some who will claim it was you who set the wheels in motion which inevitably led to the plague."

"I don't want to be a source of contention. People have enough to deal with without me. Perhaps it's best if I leave."

"I won't try to stop you, but I think you've been alone long enough. Give the people of Salem a chance to accept you. After all, you're no longer unique. No one hasn't lost at least one family member to the plague, and in some cases, entire families have been wiped out. That you have been able to survive on your own for over a year may be essential to our survival."

Tobias remembers his dream of pulling the four rivers of the Great Valley forward, his selves joining as the rivers merge into one until all unite as one and people come down to drink from the waters. "Very well, but if

Micah or Silas lives, they or some member of the Council of Elders or Order of Priests shall act in positions of authority."

"Good, that'll help to calm people's fears about you. But don't think I've forgotten about your supposed madness, because I haven't. And what's more, I don't believe it. I believe there are things you are unwilling or unable to tell me, and for now, I can live with that. Right now, I need to check on my patients, and while I do, I want you to wander the caravan and renew friendships. After I finish my rounds, I'm going to call everyone together and discuss our return to Salem. And I want you to tell people about where you've been, what you've done, and how you survived this past year. I'm hoping this will help people welcome you back."

Tobias knows the names of all the people *created* at the same time as he, but only a few of the children's names. Few people seem to notice his presence, and even fewer choose to speak to him.

Joshua Nightwind, who didn't recognize him when he first appeared at the caravan, extends his hand. "Tobias, I'm glad you're back. I apologize for not recognizing you earlier and not stopping Micah from shooting the arrow at you when you were escaping across the Red River, but I made sure he wouldn't shoot a second. For a moment, I thought my left hook broke his jaw. When I realized I didn't, I wanted to hit him a second time, but Asher stopped me."

Tobias nods, "Thank you for that. You, me, and Asher made quite a trio." Tobias swallows, "Your wife?

Children?"

He replies with a shake of his head; a young boy pulls at Joshua's pants leg. Joshua picks him up like he was no more than a feather. The boy is crying and leans into Joshua's shoulder. Joshua brushes away a tear, and talking quietly and calmly, "I didn't break my promise. I didn't go far. Let's find your mommy and sister and see what we can do to help." Joshua grins, "I may have lost my family, but that doesn't mean I'm alone."

As Tobias walks through the caravan, staring into the survivors' grief-stricken faces, he tries to imagine where they'll find the strength to carry on. He wonders if it wouldn't have been kinder and more merciful if he hadn't returned and all had died. But then, he sees a woman nurse a child that's not hers, and a man holding two young girls, one on each knee while smiling, with tears streaming down both cheeks. Everywhere he looks, he sees love expressed in simple acts of kindness and compassion, and remembering Joshua's last words, Tobias whispers, "Forgive me. I was wrong. I'm glad so many survived."

After supper, Miriam calls everyone into a large open area created by the wagons being drawn together into a tight circle.

"Friends and neighbors, the plague will soon be history. As hard as it was to watch your loved ones die, it'll be just as hard to accept that you will live. Why those that died had to die while others were allowed to live must always remain a mystery until the day our spirits return into God's presence. I know it will be challenging to find the strength and courage to continue, but we must find it for our children's sake. Life in Salem will never be the same, but that doesn't mean that we can't make it what it once was—our home.

"As all know by now, Tobias Whitefield, not I, is responsible for the cure that ended the plague. We should all rejoice that God inspired him to return. I know some are angry that he didn't return sooner. But the fact that he didn't, I think, is more the responsibility of God, who knew what was happening, than Tobias, who did not. I've asked Tobias to say a few words about where he's been and how he survived."

Tobias finds Joshua in the crowd and draws courage from knowing that he has at least one friend among the assembled group.

"Looking back over the past year, I traveled north through a desolate country I named the Tangled Hills because it's easy to become lost and confused. Eventually, I stumbled upon a wide valley with a large lake. In an overhang beside the lake, I built a house. I survived by collecting a wide variety of edible plants and supplemented my diet by hunting and fishing.

"The hardest part of surviving was not finding food or staying warm; it was living alone."

Tobias pauses, so far everything he's said is somewhat truthful, but now? Tobias swallows and takes a deep breath.

"I know many don't understand how I could learn to make such a complicated cure when I was sick with the plague. The answer is, I don't know. I remember waking sick, delirious, and afraid I was going to die. As I said, I collected plants, many I didn't know. In desperation, I...I don't know what I did. Either I got lucky, or God guided my hands, knowing that this day would come. I really don't know.

"During my time away, I've discovered things about myself and faced challenges like those you now face, challenges I didn't think it possible to overcome, but I did. I return, asking nothing more than the chance to prove that I am what Miriam thinks I can be—an asset to the community. Let it be known that I ask no special favors or seek special privileges; I am willing to serve the community in any way I can."

Joshua nods, and Daniel Tallgrass disappears from the crowd's back, talking to two other men.

When Miriam leaves for her evening rounds, Tobias returns to the Sorrow Tree and begins playing his flute.

After a while, Miriam comes to him with a pot of water, a razor, and scissors. "Whoever has been cutting your hair has been doing a terrible job."

Tobias shrugs, "You're the first person in more than a year to complain."

They both laugh.

"How much of what you told everybody is true?"

"I told the only truth possible."

"Do you think you can rebuild your place in the community based on a lie?"

"That's why I think I should leave. Within the Great Valley, life is simple. It revolves around God and living according to the *Holy Book of Life*, but outside the Great

Valley, truth is complicated and dangerous. Since leaving Salem, I've lost count of how many times I nearly died. Was it luck that I survived? Or was it divine intervention that saved me? I don't know. But what I do know is that after each time I should have died, I changed. My knowledge and understanding of how to live is no longer based upon what I saw and heard upon the Final Day of Creation or the *Holy Book of Life* but comes from knowing how to listen, and seeing myself not as the greatest of God's creations but as his least. I won't say more, but after saying what I have, do you still want me to return?"

"Yes. If Asher were here, he'd welcome you back. He told me about the last night when Micah was in pursuit of you. He said you had hidden beneath a rock ledge less than a hundred feet from their camp. And that night, during his watch with Joshua, he watched you hobble off into the night, with a badly sprained ankle, using your bow for a crutch.

"When he saw how much you hurt, yet how determined you were to remain free, he and Joshua conspired right then and there that Micah wasn't going to stop you. He said when they followed your trail to the Red River's Floodplain, the vines that were entwined in the deadfall rose up hissing and thrashing after being trod upon by the horses, spooking them. Then Joshua thought Micah might give up and let you be. But when he saw that wasn't going to happen, Asher figured the horse's frightened whinnies would give you more than enough time to hide. But Asher hadn't counted on how exhausted and hurting you were, so when he saw you push the log into the river and jump on, it ripped open his heart. He never forgave himself for not noticing you had left your bow and arrows behind before Micah did.

"Asher said that as he watched you float away, he thought the best part of what it meant to live in Salem was leaving. And from that moment on, Asher never trusted Micah. He felt Micah thought himself superior to everyone because God chose him to be High Priest.

"I don't know, maybe Asher exaggerated your importance to Salem because you were such good friends, but nothing's been the same since you left.

"So, yes, I want you to return, and I hope that in time you'll learn to trust me enough to reveal what you think you must hide. Sharing your burden will make it lighter to carry." Miriam smirks. "Besides, we have a more pressing problem."

An hour later, Tobias is clean-shaven with his hair stylishly cut. Miriam, her eyes closed, her words slurring with near sleep, leans against Tobias's shoulder. She sighs contentedly. "Last night, I heard you play your flute. I found the music beautiful, but also quite sad. Will you play for me?"

Back on Earth, when he was Erik and Miriam was Jenny, a moment like this would lead to a night of slow sensuality building into an ecstatic climax that would leave them both physically exhausted.

Tobias plays a single tune, *Tambour's Heartache*. When he finishes, he wipes a tear from her cheek.

Miriam whispers, "That was beautiful, but so sad. Do you know any cheerful songs?"

She turns her face to Tobias. He shakes his head.

Miriam closes her eyes and touches her chin to her chest. "Now that you've returned and the plague will soon be a memory and we can all return to Salem, have you asked what next?"

"No, and neither should you. You have been so entangled with trying to save lives, you haven't had time to grieve your own loss. I know you think you have developed a callousness in your heart to hide your grief as you helped others, but now it's time for you to remember all that you've lost. Don't look to me to find a shortcut or easy way out of it. If I have learned anything since I've been away, it's that grief and heartache aren't just in the mind, but are as real as any tree or rock and must be encountered in much the same way."

Miriam sighs. "You made the flute?"

"No, I mean… yes, of course, I made the flute."

"It's beautiful, but I don't recognize the wood. Asher is…I mean, was a carpenter, so I should know what it is."

"It doesn't grow around here."

After a lengthy silence, Tobias senses Miriam is falling asleep. He rouses her. "Come, let's get you back so people will know where to find you. Also, I've decided to leave at first light and return to Salem. Your caravan won't leave for a couple of days, which means I'll arrive in time to assess what needs doing before you arrive."

Tobias stands and reaches down to give Miriam a hand up, but she ignores the offer. "Go. What do I care?"

Miriam stomps off, leaving Tobias to wonder what just happened.

• • •

Tobias's first thought upon waking beneath the Sorrow Tree is of Miriam. By the time he reaches her wagon, she's finished her morning rounds and waits for him to come to her.

"I'm sorry I got upset with you last night. I overreacted. You're right, I have been so concerned about others' welfare," her shoulders slump, "I haven't taken care of myself. I'm exhausted from being the one everyone looks to for answers. Perhaps instead of going to Salem ahead of the caravan, you could take charge and let me rest."

"No, it wouldn't work. I've seen it in everyone's faces—how much they admire, respect, and trust you. You need to be strong for a few more days. Once back in Salem, you can become Miriam, the woman, the grieving mother and widow, and community healer. Still, I would like your permission to return to Salem ahead of the caravan. I can begin rounding up livestock and see what I can do to make the homecoming easier."

"You don't need my permission."

"Perhaps not, but as you're the caravan leader, I would prefer it."

"Yes, of course, you have my permission, and if you wish to borrow a horse or want others to go with you…"

"No, I prefer to go on foot and alone. As difficult as it will be for everyone to return, it will be doubly so for me."

Miriam looks past Tobias. "Go quickly."

Tobias does as Miriam asks, but less than a minute later, when he turns to give a final wave, he sees Miriam

154

going toe to toe with Daniel Tallgrass, who is jabbing his finger towards Tobias.

For a moment, Tobias considers returning and coming to Miriam's defense, but decides doing so would only agitate Daniel and undermine Miriam's authority. Besides, Miriam has proven she is more than capable of taking care of herself.

Mid-afternoon of the third day after leaving the caravan, Tobias arrives at the tree Rebecca named the Leaving Tree, the spot where Asher, Miriam's husband, rode out to meet Tobias with the message that Rebecca was having trouble birthing their child and the place he spent the first night after fleeing Salem.

Placing his hand against the tree's bark, Tobias whispers, "I have come full circle. As much as I have longed for this moment, I'm afraid now that it's arrived. I once thought the dream I had of the four rivers of the Great Valley uniting in me and the people coming down to drink meant I was returning with something beneficial for the people of Salem, like the knowledge of how to enter the Circle of Always Becoming. But now I wonder if the dream is a warning the people of Salem will seek to draw their life from me, that I'll be viewed as their savior and expected to solve their problems, heal their wounds, and restore Salem to how it was before the plague.

"I know I promised Miriam I would stay until Salem's survival is assured, and I will. I only hope that during that time, I can show them who their true savior is: their faith in God and living by the laws and commandments of the *Holy Book of Life*. I know these are based on a lie, but what does it matter if believing it is so helps them survive? Perhaps Butterfly was wrong. Perhaps sometimes people do need a lie to give them courage."

Tobias leans into the tree and spreads his arms wide. He whispers, "When I die, if my spirit is allowed to find its tree, perhaps it will find its way here."

• • •

Tobias enters Salem in the thickening dusk and stops beside the graves of Rebecca and Naomi. Dropping to his knees, Tobias traces with a finger the letters carved into the gravestone laid flat across the grave's length.

"Unlike Erik and Corvus, who were free to choose who they loved, I had no choice but to love you. And yet, judging by the amount of pain I felt when you died, our love was real."

With one arm flung across the gravestone, Tobias lies on his stomach and lets his tears flow unchecked. By the time Tobias rolls onto his back, the sky is dark. Selene is setting just as Luna is rising.

*What is it about returning to Salem that suddenly makes me want to start believing in their God again? Is it all the memories I've made here? Is it something in the air, or my desire to belong? Whatever it is, I've seen too much and done too much for the spell to last.*

As he walks away, Tobias thinks, *This isn't right. There must have been fifty, a hundred, or more who died before Salem was abandoned. If they're not buried here, then where?*

Hurrying past the Temple to the north-south street that borders Town Square Park's west edge, he stops and gives a long stare in both directions.

*I knew Salem would be deserted. I knew there wouldn't be any lights in windows or cattle lowing or horses neighing, but I wasn't expecting all the broken pots, scattered papers, smashed cradles, soiled cloth dolls, children's shoes—all the discarded bits of lives. As impossible as it was to hear the crying when I came upon the caravan, how much worse it must have been when they left with only their belief in God and trust in Miriam to find a cure. If it's possible to taste sadness and despair, it's now. Even the trees have forgotten how to rustle their leaves.*

Without giving thought as to where he's going or why, Tobias walks the dozen blocks north toward the livestock pens. *If my spirit was too heavy before to enter the Circle of Always Becoming, what chance do I have now?*

*What's wrong with people? Why couldn't they have just said no? If I had been here when the Land Bountiful was discovered, would my voice have made a difference? Would I have been able to stop the madness? Or was the plague something that needed to happen?*

When he reaches the empty livestock pens on the north end of town, he thinks, *There's so much that needs doing. My returning early won't make any difference.*

Heading back towards Town Square Park, Tobias passes by Miriam's house and is startled by the sound of something being knocked over. A glance around is enough to convince himself that it must have been some animal or gust of wind.

Continuing to his house, Tobias finds the windows

shuttered, a fate soon to be shared by half or perhaps more of the houses.

As he approaches the park, where he intends to spend the night, Tobias is again startled, this time by a flickering candle flame that disappears only to reappear. Tobias, chasing after it like he did the Goddess during his first visit to the Ethereal Glade, realizes he is being led up Temple Hill and to the Temple's entrance, where the candle comes to rest.

Stopping in front of the door, Tobias picks up the candle and looks around for the person who had carried it there. Seeing no one, Tobias blows out its flame. "Whoever you are, you don't need to be afraid. The plague is over. Join me in the park. Let's talk. I've food to spare."

After a long minute of waiting and neither seeing nor hearing anything, Tobias spins about and leans his ear against the door. Something or someone is moving inside the Temple. But as he leans against the door, he thinks, *The only thing I've ever smelled as putrid and pungent as what is coming out of the Temple is a rotting corpse.*

Tobias pauses as he grasps the Temple door's handle and quietly chuckles. What, if anything, he wonders, will happen when he enters the Temple he nearly single-handedly built for a God that he now knows is a lie? He smiles as he remembers what Butterfly had said when he told her of the Temple: "Why would God live in such a place?"

After taking a steadying breath, Tobias flings the door open. Gagging, he drops to his knees, his head touching the stone floor, fighting the urge to vomit.

For nearly seven years, Tobias worked constructing the Temple. He knows its every inch so well that he doesn't wait for his eyes to adjust to the darkness but bulls his way through the stench to the second set of doors and without a second's pause throws both doors open wide. Forcing himself to his full height, Tobias thrusts out his chest and marches steadily down the broad, shallow steps to the low wall enclosing the Holy of Holies, the Whitened Rock. He then does something which no man has ever done, nor would he dare do if he still believed in Salem's God. He climbs to the rock's pinnacle.

As his eyes adjust to the near-total darkness, Tobias sees the outline of thirty, perhaps forty, men, women, and children in different horror-stricken poses, all dead.

A voice out of the darkness asks, "Do you like my work?"

Tobias thunders with the voice of the Sunfisher, "Who are you?"

"I am Micah Skylark, and you are Tobias, coward, and blasphemer! How dare you defile the Whitened Rock! The punishment is death! And I, God's chosen to be High Priest, shall mete out your punishment. But first, I must know why you returned."

"I am here to begin preparations for the return of many hundreds of survivors."

"That's not possible! God has ordained all are guilty. All must die!"

Tobias points. "How can a baby be guilty?"

"How can a baby not be guilty, being born into this world the product of two imperfect people?"

"Born imperfect, always in a state of falling, man strives unto his dying breath to raise himself up."

"Don't quote scriptures to me! No man shall be my judge! Neither shall any man be allowed to live. It is my sworn and sacred duty."

"I, who cured the plague, shall bear witness against you and proclaim your madness an affront to God. The many hundred that still live shall hold you accountable by the laws of man and God."

"You have no power over me!"

Tobias leaps off the Whitened Rock, jumps over the low stone wall, and races up the steps, but by the time he gets to the entranceway, Micah Skylark, High Priest, and mass murderer has vanished into the night.

Returning to the Whitened Rock, Tobias speaks from its summit to the putrefying bodies of people he once knew. "I have no comfort to offer, and knowing the truth as I do about the God for whom this Temple was built, I know He has none to offer. However, I can promise you the death of Micah Skylark either at my hands or those that survived the plague, but is that what you need?

"Is it possible that upon your death you remembered past the computer programming and awakened to re-membering your life on Earth? If so, do you feel as lost and alone as I did when I remembered? You may not have been born into this world, but here you have died. And here is where, if anything happens to your immor-tal soul, will happen.

"The best I can promise is that you shall not be forgotten or abandoned."

Tobias takes Butterfly's flute and plays until the first rays of sunlight shining through the open doors pierce the Temple's interior gloom. He then hastens down the hill to the Community Center which fronts Town Square Park on the north. It takes four trips to get enough cloth sheets to wrap each body tightly. By noon, the last person is shrouded.

His grisly task done, Tobias wonders, what would Butterfly's people do to somebody as evil as Micah, before hacking their body into pieces and crushing their skull?

Hurrying to his house, Tobias breaks in the front door. As far as he can tell, everything is how it was when he left. After filling a large tub with water, Tobias strips and, with water so cold it raises goosebumps, scours his entire body so hard it glows pink, then dresses in a change of clothes he left when he fled Salem.

• • •

Having spent the night among rotting corpses, Tobias has no urge to eat, and no desire for sleep. Instead, he decides to check on the food surplus warehouses built adjacent to the cultivated fields on the town's southern outskirts. If they are intact, Salem's survival is guaranteed for at least two, maybe three years, and he is under no long-term obligation to stay.

Halfway across Town Square Park's grassy expanse, dotted with trees behind which Micah might lie in ambush, Tobias stops and yells loud enough for his voice to echo. "Micah, if you can hear me, know I am not afraid because I know that to ensure what must happen happens, God has ordained that I must live and you must die. If this were not so, all God would have needed to do to make sure everyone died was to prevent my return. Although you may hide in shadows and seek to kill me by ambush, you are doomed to failure."

Tobias turns a tight circle, listening for the slightest sound, looking for the slightest movement. When he sees no one, he walks with false bravado along the southern road and stops a half-mile outside of town.

The warehouses have been reduced to a still-warm, smoldering ash pile.

Micah steps out from behind a tree, holding a bow with an arrow in place, pointing downward. "Do you like what I've done?"

"Thanks to you, Salem's people will have a difficult struggle to survive the winter."

"No one should live; all must die."

Micah is standing on the edge of a broad, shallow ditch thirty feet from Tobias.

"Micah, you've changed. You're filthy, and your clothes are dirty. Where are your shiny black shoes and perfectly manicured hands? When was the last time you bathed, shaved, or combed your hair?"

Micah shrugs. "And what about you? You smell of rotting corpses."

Tobias closes the distance between them by three steps but stops when Micah raises the bow. "The *Holy*

*Book of Life*, the copy written by God's hand, is gone from the Temple. Do you have it?"

"Yes, I took it and have hidden it away. I burned the other two copies, but God's handwritten copy cannot be burned or cut with a knife. How strange."

Tobias thinks, *Thirty-third century Earth technology at work*. "What else would you expect from an all-powerful, all-knowing God, capable of striking you down at any moment?"

Another two steps before Micah moves the bow into firing position. Tobias stops and raises his hands and thinks that the problem with using a bow is that it's not effective up close. He was lucky to get the shot off when the wild boar charged him in the clearing below the Jaguar people's home.

Micah breaks into a broad grin. "And yet He doesn't. What does that say to you?"

Tobias shrugs, then, bending low, rushes Micah, sending him stumbling backward, still grasping the bow. Tobias jumps into the ditch and steps on Micah's hand.

Micah relaxes, lets go of the bow, and grins. "You think you've won, but you haven't. You'll see. I'll be the death of you yet."

Tobias picks Micah up with one hand and sends him staggering forward.

Micah screams, "My ankle! I think it's broken."

"Miriam can check it out when she returns. Until then, use your bow for a crutch. When you chased after me after I left Salem, I sprained my ankle and used a bow for a crutch. It's too bendy to work well. Still, it's better than nothing."

It takes much longer than it should to arrive at the Office of the Elders that fronts onto the eastern edge of Town Square Park, where they descend into the basement.

Tobias pushes Micah into a cell, perhaps the very cell he might have called home if Micah had had his way in the days following Rebecca's death, then closes and double bars the door. He looks through a small hole at eye level.

"If you're lucky, I'll remember to bring you food and water that's not poisoned."

Micah rushes the door. Tobias takes a step back.

"You can't do this! I am Micah Skylark; I am the Chosen One. I obey God and no other."

As Tobias's footsteps die away, Micah's voice grows into a scream, as if he's in terrible agony.

Tobias spends the rest of the day driving a few of the closest cows back into the pens and filling the feed trough with hay.

An hour after sundown, Tobias watches the flickering torch-light of Miriam's returning caravan following along the western road.

A few minutes later, a rider, Joshua Nightwind, appears. "Silas and twenty-three more are just a few miles away to the east. I'm to let Miriam know."

Tobias points to a line of flickering torches, the glowing orange snake of his dream. "Miriam should arrive at about the same time, but she mustn't enter past the Temple. You need to tell both to return through the north entrance."

Joshua glances back towards where he had just come, then towards the caravan led by Miriam. "Are you going to tell me why?"

"No, I'll tell everybody at once."

Joshua nods then urges his horse into a fast canter towards the caravan led by Miriam.

Miriam arrives just before Silas. "So, what's happening? Why did you want us to come this way?"

"Just be glad I returned early."

Miriam and Tobias watch Daniel Tallgrass hurry to the approaching caravan's lead wagon and help Silas Windcatcher, the Chief Elder, step down from the wagon. Silas hobbles over to where Miriam and Tobias are waiting.

Silas offers his hand, which Tobias takes, and returns the grasp with no more strength than is offered.

Silas grins a toothy smile. "I understand I have you to thank for saving my life. I was hours from dying when the medicine arrived." Silas acknowledges Miriam with a nod. "Daniel Tallgrass just told me of the extraordinary job of leadership that you exhibited in taking charge of the caravan."

Miriam looks to Tobias, then back to Silas. "I'm sure that's not all he told you."

All expression vanishes from Silas' face.

Ignoring the unspoken undercurrent, Tobias says, "What's important is that when I arrived in Salem last night, I discovered why none of the Order of Priests is here to join us. Within the Temple are the bodies of all the priests and their families. All except Micah Skylark, who is insane and poisoned everyone. Last night I confronted him, and he admitted it. This morning, when I checked on the surplus storage warehouses, I found they had been reduced to ashes. When I again confronted Micah, he freely admitted he set fire to the warehouses. He also admitted that he stole the *Holy Book of Life* written by God's hand and has burned all other copies. I apprehended Micah and locked him in the holding cell beneath the Council of Elders' offices. Anything more, I leave to the Council of Elders."

Silas winces and appears to bend beneath the revelation's weight, then asks, "Anything else I should know before we enter Salem?"

"That's the worst. Obviously, there is so much to do all at once, there's…"

Silas casts a wry glance at Miriam. "Thank you, Tobias, that's for tomorrow. For now, everyone shall return to their houses."

Miriam barks, "No! Tonight, everyone shall go to the community center, where I can make sure that all are well-fed and no one is alone."

Silas scowls, takes a deep breath, and sighs. "Yes, of course, you're right. Plus, it will facilitate getting a complete census of all who live so we can best assign jobs."

When at last people are lying on makeshift beds and drifting off to sleep, Silas seeks Tobias out. "Let's get one thing straight right from the start. I'm in charge, not you. I give the orders, not you. You can't just return and expect to take control. Unfortunately for you, I am God's chosen to be Chief Elder, God's chosen to lead the people of Salem, and as long as I live, I, not you, are in command."

"I have no desire to lead, much less command. It's my only desire to help the people of Salem survive the winter."

"Good, then in the morning, you can begin removing the bodies from the Temple and undertake the task of cleaning it. Unfortunately, I cannot give you help; everyone else will be engaged in important work."

"As you wish."

"Hmm, yes, and of course, we'll need a new Order of Priests. But that can wait. I wonder if there's anything in the *Holy Book of Life* preventing me from taking on the role of High Priest?" Silas smiles. "I must look, assuming we ever find it."

He walks away, then stops. "Perhaps you'd like the job of a priest, temporarily?"

Silas emphasized *temporarily* with such undisguised disgust that Tobias could only smile. "Yes, I'd like that. If the *Holy Book of Life* can't be found, a new copy will have to be made from the combined memory of everyone that lives. Together, I am sure we can reconstruct the text word for word."

"Yes, yes, a vital and time-consuming occupation. By the way, I questioned Micah. As you said, he is quite crazed, but as soon as I opened the door to check on him, he claimed you badly beat him. Micah overpowered me, and ran away. I chased after him, but he was too fast."

Tobias grins. *Micah was too fast on a badly sprained ankle?* "Then he couldn't have been too badly hurt. Micah will struggle to find food. No doubt, he'll try to steal what he needs, so I recommend a full-time watch on our food supplies…"

"Yes, yes, already done, now leave the running of the town to me."

Silas stomps off as Miriam comes over and stands beside Tobias. "What did Silas want?"

"He wants me to know he is in charge, and for me to keep me out of his way. Somehow he thinks he has the authority to make me a priest, and my first act as a priest is to single-handedly remove the bodies from the Holy Temple, then thoroughly clean it."

"No, he can't expect you do to that all by yourself. In the morning, I'll…."

"No, don't. I don't intend to challenge Silas's author-ity, first because the bodies need to be removed and the Temple cleaned, and second because I don't want there to be a division in Salem about whom people feel loyalty towards."

Miriam kisses Tobias on the cheek and whispers in his ear, "When did you get so wise?"

• • •

When Tobias wakes, Miriam's gone. She and a dozen women are readying breakfast. Two girls, ages five and three, and a boy of eighteen months are sleeping nearby. These are the children for whom Miriam has accepted responsibility. How many times during the night had one or all, feeding off each other's fears, woke, crying and kicking, their little hands balled into fists of rage?

But in the soft morning light, their faces are peaceful. But what, Tobias wonders, does he offer them? He never had children, and while he remembers Erik's childhood on Earth, what he remembers he wouldn't wish on anyone.

Silas, accompanied by Daniel Tallgrass, is methodically making his way through the sprawling confusion of adults and children. Daniel takes notes about each conversation. When at last they get to Tobias, Silas smiles his toothy smile. "And where will you be staying?"

"At Miriam's, I suppose. She'll need help with the children."

"So, not at your house?"

"No. My house would take considerable time and effort to make livable."

"Quite right. There are, however, many houses made vacant by recent events."

"True, but Miriam, as a healer and in charge of three children, can use my help."

Silas moves his jaw around like he's chewing on an idea. "You're right; three children might be too much for Miriam.

"Last night, we discussed your duties. Questions?"

"Yes. Where did the priests bury the bodies?"

"They didn't. A mile along the eastern road, there's a pit. I determined burning to be the most efficient means of disposal.

"Any idea how long it'll take to clean the Temple?"

"I'm hoping two days to get rid of the gore, then..."

"So long? Still, I suppose it can't be helped. Anything else?"

"Yes. Yesterday you asked me to take on the role of a priest. I think Joshua Nightwind is a better choice. I'll gladly assist..."

"Joshua?" Silas turns to Daniel. "Did you get that? Joshua Nightwind. Of course, he'll have to agree, but I think you are right; he is rather boring and serious-minded."

The oldest girl wakes, rubs her eyes, takes one look at Silas, and runs to Tobias. "Where's Mommy? Where's *Miree?*"

Tobias flinches. Miree? He has to swallow before he can say the name. In the language of the Jaguar people, Miree means nobody, but Miriam is not nobody.

"Miree is getting our breakfast. Let's wake the others and then, well, you know, do what we must before washing hands and combing hair."

Silas smiles down at the little girl. "Yes, well, I see you have your hands full. Keep me updated."

The little girl is on the verge of tears when she leaps to her feet and yells, "Miree!" She grabs Miriam's knees, then bursts into tears.

Miriam chuckles. "You've got a lot to learn about taking care of children, but you've got time, and I am a very patient teacher. I saw you talking to Silas; everything okay?"

Tobias shrugs, "I got him to ask Joshua Nightwind to take on the job of a priest."

Miriam hugs the little girl, who is both smiling and crying. "I've got plenty to keep me busy, but I'll manage lunch and bring it to you at the Temple…"

"No, don't. I'll be in and out of there, and besides, I doubt I'll be able to eat anything after spending hours in that awful…" He glances down at the little girl. "Enough said."

Miriam picks up the young girl. "Yes, enough said."

After breakfast, people mill about. Tobias, watching over the children, shudders to see Miriam and Silas engaged in a vigorous discussion, their faces inches apart. When at last they separate, Silas whispers something to Daniel, who meanders through the crowd talking to all the men.

Silas comes over to Tobias and snarls, "You've got your orders…"

Miriam interrupts Silas. "A few minutes wasted now will save hours later. People need direction, not orders."

Tobias asks, "Do you need me to watch the kids while you get everything up and running?"

Miriam sighs. "No, we'll be fine."

*Fine? That,* Tobias thinks, *is the last thing anyone will be for a very long time.*

Before going to the Temple, Tobias goes first to the stables, where he hitches two horses to a long, narrow wagon with tall sides that should have been used by the priests.

Returning to the Temple, Tobias parks the wagon as close to the front door as he can, then stares into the darkness softened by sunlight streaming through the Temple's front door, which he left open to lessen the stench. But, afraid of scavenging animals that despite the bodies being enshrouded might feast on the corpses, which among the Jaguar people is the accepted practice and hastens the body's return into nature, he left the second set of doors shut.

*Does the difference between the two traditions come from the Jaguar people seeing themselves as the least of God's creation and Salem's people viewing themselves as the epitome of God's work? And given a choice, which would I choose for myself?* He shudders away the thought. *What happens to my body will depend on whether I'm among people or nature.*

Slowly and deliberately, Tobias dismounts from the wagon and walks with a steady gait, the vision of what awaits before his eyes, into the outer chamber. When he reaches the double doors leading into the Holy of Holies, Tobias doesn't hesitate but flings them wide. He doesn't turn from the stench but lets it hit him with the power and force of the wind when he first climbed to Burial Cairn Ridge. Unlike then, when he had to force himself forward, now he bulls his way forward and stops just outside the low wall surrounding the Whitened Stone.

Feeling light-headed, Tobias sits on the wall and bends his head between his knees. *Is the air poisoned? Or is it just disgust in its most pure form that makes me feel this way?*

Biting his upper lip hard enough to rekindle his anger, Tobias growls, "No one should have to do what I must do." His eyes rest upon the nearest shrouded body, a child small enough that it might still have been nursing. Tobias carefully places his hands under the body, making sure the head is properly supported, smiles down on it, and rocks it back and forth, like he would have held his child if his union with Rebecca had been blessed.

Turning to face not the north where the Yellow Eye shines unseen but west to Butterfly's home, he whispers, "Never before has my spirit hung so heavy. How shall I ever enter the Circle?"

"Tambour, you confuse what was with what is. What you hold is not a child but something which contained the child's spirit. By letting the beasts of the ground and air eat our loved ones' bodies, we remember this truth.

"Tambour, what do you want for the child you hold? A child who knew nothing but love? Revenge will not restore its life.

"What do you want for the man who killed her? The pain-filled, lingering death of one who kills a jaguar?

"Tambour, what do you think is better? Anger quenched by revenge or anger quenched with compassion? That the man must and will die for what he has done, there can be no doubt; the question is, will you let his death poison your spirit?"

Tobias carries the child to the wagon and places her behind the wagon seat. *She's so small and all alone. How can Butterfly ask me to feel compassion for the inhuman monster capable of killing a helpless innocent?*

By careful arrangement, Tobias fits ten bodies into the wagon bed without having to stack one on top of another like he might quarried stone.

As he drives the wagon along the south side of Town Square Park, Tobias sees more than two dozen people on their way somewhere to do whatever Silas has ordered them to do. But when he realizes he sees no children, he smiles and thinks, *The children are safe, cared for, and nurtured as best as Miriam can manage.*

When Tobias arrives at the burning pit fifteen minutes later, his strength flows out of him. Whatever he was expecting, it wasn't an irregular hole forty feet in diameter, varying in depth from four to eight feet with sloping sides and a massive dirt pile heaped along the rim on three sides. Its black clay bottom, covered with ash and partially burned bones, turned to gray paste by recent rains and burned red. Tobias releases a sigh of relief as he sees enough logs for one last burn stacked along the pit's western edge.

As he stares into the pit, Tobias imagines Silas yelling, "Don't waste time being careful. Just toss them. They're dead. Nothing's going to hurt them." Except it wouldn't have been Silas, but Micah, who was directing the burning. As much as he might not like Micah for forcing him to leave Salem, Tobias wonders how Micah or any man could deal with so much death. *No doubt, Micah spent hours talking to God, pleading with God for an answer, but when no response came from a God who does not exist, was that enough to poison his mind?*

Before doing anything, Tobias imagines Rebecca carefully stacking wood in a potter's kiln, and pays close attention to where she places the pots to ensure that all are evenly and completely fired.

The pit's sides are too steep to allow the wagon, so he must content himself with a single horse to move logs too heavy for him to budge into position. It takes until early afternoon to lay the foundation for a three-tier lattice and lay the first bodies on the bottom tier.

Joshua stops Tobias on his third trip through the town square. "Miriam told me what Silas has you doing. When I finish, I'll come help."

"No, you've got someone waiting, depending on you. I don't."

"Not really, I just help wherever I can."

"And that, from what I saw the first night I arrived at the caravan, is your true calling, which is why I asked Silas to talk to you about taking on the role of priest and conducting the Ceremony of Remembrance and Release."

"As I told him, I'll do it, but it makes me uncomfortable. I mean, if God had wanted me to be a priest, He would have made me one from the beginning."

"If He had, you'd be dead."

Joshua looks down at his feet, then into Tobias's eyes. "But what do I know about being a priest?"

"What does anybody know except those who are dead? But more important than knowing the rules and rituals, you have the most important requirement: compassion. Besides, haven't you taken on a priest's role by doing what you are already doing—bringing help and comfort wherever you're needed?"

Joshua looks to the ground, swallows, looks up, and nods. "Thank you. Your confidence means a lot."

Tobias gives the reins a shake. As the wagon jolts forward, Tobias thinks, *Joshua will make an excellent priest.*

Long after most people have sought their beds, Tobias stacks the last bodies in the upper tier of the lattice-work, then returns the horses and wagon to the stables.

Two hours later, Tobias finishes stuffing every straw, twig, and scrap of wood he can find beneath the bottom tier, then tosses a torch onto the kindling and retreats to the pit's rim. He stands mesmerized by the fire's dance, punctuated with pops and sparks. Large red embers float like leaves, propelled upward by the swirling heat and smoke.

*Micah Skylark, an insane mass murderer; Daniel Tallgrass, a grief-crazed paranoid; and Silas Windcatcher, a power-obsessed petty tyrant. How many others are in similar states? Like the little children he slept beside last night, how many others will feed off each other's fear and anger and become more unstable?*

Tobias shakes his head to clear the thought and re-members Butterfly's words: *"Think no farther than the length a single note from the music stick hangs in the air."*

As the fire blazes and Tobias gazes into its heart, he doesn't notice when an arm slips through his, nor does he hear the gentle whisper, "I'm here."

Then, under her breath, "Ew, the smell, how do you stand it?" In the flickering firelight, Miriam watches shadows play across Tobias's face, revealing secrets she cannot decipher. She shivers and leans into him. "I can't stay because of the children I, or rather we, have taken in. Will you come home with me?"

"The magic bloom. I must stay with it."

Miriam mouths, "Magic bloom?" A question for another time. "Just as I need someone to share my burden, so do you." She rocks forward to stand on tiptoes and kisses his cheek. "You're not alone."

After a lengthy silence, Miriam leaves, pausing only once to look back. She wonders what he sees in the flames that he can't turn away from.

Tobias sleeps beside the fire and, in the morning, fills in the Burning Pit to a depth of several feet.

Returning to the Temple, Tobias closes the door, lights candles and sticks of incense on the four corners of the Holy of Holies, and strips. It is easier to get blood and gore off of skin than clothes.

Taking the first of several bucketfuls of soapy water, Tobias gets on his hands and knees and begins scrubbing. It takes all day and well into the night to cleanse the area where he found the bodies. After finishing, he dresses and wanders down Temple Hill toward Town Square Park.

The streets are empty. A cool breeze blows out of an approaching storm. The first few raindrops surprise Tobias. He holds out a hand and looks up, and a large drop hits below his left eye. He wipes the water out of his eye. *Am I crying?*

"There you are." Miriam walks, cradling a boy in one arm while holding the hand of a young girl who holds her younger sister's hand. "Have you eaten?"

Tobias stares without seeing. He jerks his head.

"You must be starving. You haven't eaten for nearly two days. Come, I saved your dinner."

Tobias looks into her tense, smiling face, but his mind is filled with bloated, maggot-filled corpses and the smell of burning flesh.

Tobias doesn't awaken until late the next afternoon.

When he does, it's to the sound of Silas Windcatcher's voice. "Where's Tobias?"

Miriam answers. "He's here."

"Wake him! We need to talk."

Tobias staggers out of the bedroom, wrapped in only a towel. "I'm awake."

Silas scowls at Tobias and glares at Miriam. "People have been talking. They've been asking where you've been and what you've been doing." His glance alternates between Miriam and Tobias. "I don't know what to tell them."

"Tell them I've disposed of the bodies inside the Temple, filled the Burning Pit, and cleaned away all trace of the abomination."

Silas waves away what Tobias is saying. "Some people want you to be High Priest. I think it a terrible idea."

"I agree. I don't want to be on an equal footing with you."

"You wouldn't be. The High Priest is not my equal."

"After I finish cleaning the Temple, I would like to begin work on a memorial at the Burning Pit site. On it, we can engrave the names of everyone who died."

Silas snarls. "I've talked to Joshua. He says he talked to you, and together you'll put together some sort of Ceremony of Remembrance and Release."

"Yes."

"Good! Just make it clear that neither you nor Joshua are anything special. I think the ceremony should be short and to the point, held the day after tomorrow after sundown so everyone can put in a full day's work.

Afterward, I doubt anyone will be of much use. Then, yes, go to the quarry and spend all the time you need to gather your precious stone."

Tobias smiles. "If you're sure I'm not needed elsewhere. I don't know how the new Order of Priests will be selected, but I've been thinking, maybe the High Priest should be a woman."

"No! God on the Final Day of Creation made the Chief Elder and all of his Council and the High Priest and all the Order of Priests men, and I can't see any reason for the change."

During the following days, Tobias spends most of his time cleaning every inch of the Temple. In the evening, he stays with Anna, Abigail, and Andrew, while Miriam visits the people having the hardest time coping with their grief.

The first time Miriam left him alone with the children, Tobias had objected, saying, "What if something happens or they cry?"

Miriam grinned. "A big, strong, self-reliant, invincible man like you afraid of three small children? Relax. They've been fed, and if you play games with them and keep them active, they'll tire out quickly and fall asleep."

"Games? What do I know about children's games?"

"Don't worry; they'll teach you. And why not play your flute? If you can play something happy, I bet they'll wiggle and dance about and tire out even quicker, and they'll learn to see you as someone capable of having fun and not always being so serious-minded."

That first night, Miriam returns to find Tobias asleep

on the couch, holding the sleeping boy in his lap with one girl asleep on either side. She kisses him on the forehead and watches his eyes flutter open and whispers, "See, that wasn't so hard now, was it?"

Tobias hands the boy to Miriam, then follows her into the children's bedroom, carrying the oldest girl. He waits for Miriam to turn down the bedspread before returning to the living room for the other girl. Once all are tucked in, Miriam puts an arm about his waist, leans into him, and whispers, "The poor innocents will need so much. It'll take everyone's combined efforts if they are ever to be happy and live normal lives."

They return to the living room. Miriam snuggles so close to Tobias he must put an arm about her. She explains that when visiting her patients, she gives out very little medicine of any medicinal value beyond the patient's belief that it helps. She recounts stories about when people realized they were infected and could no longer be part of the group; some reacted with anger, some with resignation. But the worst was when a child was affected and neither parent was. More often than not, one parent would go with them, and once they did, they could never return. She leans harder into Tobias as she continues, "And because I was needed to find a cure when Martha got sick, Asher went with her, but it still haunts my dreams how she cried after me, and then when Gideon got sick, and by then Asher was infected, and…" Miriam bursts into tears.

Tobias holds her like he held Rebecca when she found out she was pregnant for the last time and lets her cry. It's the first time Miriam has spoken about what happened to her family.

Two days later, Joshua Nightwind walks to the top of a small platform in Town Square Park just as Luna is rising full and the sun is setting. He looks nervously about, then nods to Tobias, who begins playing *Red Tower Vision*, which, with its otherworldly sound, floats over the assembled crowd like a warm blanket on a cold night. By the time he finishes, everyone, including the children, is quiet.

Joshua begins, "Friends, we have gathered here today to say goodbye to so many loved ones. There is no one here whose heart has not been shattered by grief. I've been told that the census has been completed, and of the 896 people who lived in Salem at the coming of the plague, only 384 remain. Of those, nearly two-thirds are children. This is a time when everyone must come together as one family united by love.

"Make no mistake. I have not been called by God to be a priest, so my voice is no louder nor more directly linked to God's ear than anyone else's. I ask that each person take time to talk aloud to God to pour out your innermost thoughts and feelings and let Him know of your love for Him. Remember always that He is a God of love, and it's through His great love that a cure was discovered so all might not perish, so once again we can build Salem into a splendid city and provide a vibrant future for our children.

"And as the mountains to the west are called the Forbidden Mountains, let us also call the gorge to the east the Forbidden Gorge, forbidden only by the laws of man, and agree that no one shall pass through it except of the greatest necessity, or until the people of Salem outgrow the Great Valley many generations beyond the foreseeable future.

"At the first Ceremony of Remembrance and Release conducted to honor the passing of Rebecca and Naomi Whitefield, many people shared their remembrances of how the deceased touched their lives, but with so many deaths in such a short time, this is not possible. And so I ask each person to write a collection of remembrances of their loved ones and those friends and neighbors that touched their lives. These volumes shall be collected and provide the beginning of a library honoring all who have ever lived, so none are forgotten.

"But only part of the ceremony is Remembrance. The other part is Release, and that is the hardest task which anyone can be asked to do. Yet it's vital that each and every one in their own time and own way let go of those they've lost as a final act of love which releases the spirits of those who have died so those spirits can seek comfort. To cling to the memories of those we've lost is to live in the past, and the past is no place to live.

"We shall finish by asking Tobias to play a song he wrote the first night he arrived in Salem ahead of the caravans. It's called *Song of Sorrow and Farewell*, and I ask that as he plays, each person close their eyes, tell God of their love for those lost, and release them into His care."

Tobias plays *Tambour's Heartache*.

Joshua returns to the podium and says, "Praise God,

God is love," which the crowd echoes.

Silas arrives at Miriam's house early the next day. Tobias and Miriam stand shoulder to shoulder as Silas snarls, "Last night's ceremony was excellent, except Joshua overstepped his bounds by making civil law. Forbidden Gorge indeed! Of course, I'll have to consider the matter before acting. Undoubtedly, most people will agree with Joshua that it was the plague's source and should be avoided, but I hate giving up all the resources it contains and its access to the sea. Otherwise, Joshua did a good job. You and he should continue to work together in that capacity until I can fill the vacancies in the Council of Elders and find time to appoint priests."

Tobias nods. "Very well, but as agreed, today I leave for the quarry. I plan to return in six days. In the meantime, I think you should appoint Joshua as acting High Priest and give him instruction to reconstruct the *Holy Book of Life* from memory."

"I have someone else in mind for High Priest, but I think Joshua could begin reinventing the Holy Scriptures. By the way, were you surprised that Micah did not interrupt last night's ceremony, if only out of jealousy or anger for having his office and power stolen?"

"No, I stopped thinking or worrying about Micah the day after the caravans arrived back in Salem. Micah is either dead or, more likely, a sniveling coward afraid to take on anyone in a fair fight. I only wish that if he still lives, Micah finds out about my trip to the quarry and comes after me. If he does, all I can say is he'd better get it right the first time, because he only gets one try."

Tobias feels a warm rush. Is it possible that, just for a flicker, Silas was rattled?

• • •

This time when Tobias leaves for the quarry, it's Miriam, not Rebecca, who accompanies him to the Leaving Tree. After a lunch of cold chicken, apples, bread, and cheese, Miriam looks down at her hands in her lap. "If you're still determined to leave, there's nothing to stop you. Between what was salvaged from the warehouses Micah burned, the crops that Silas and the Elders collected before they left, and what remains to be harvested, Salem's survival is ensured for at least one year."

Tobias passes his fingers through the grass, then slowly looks up and gazes straight into Miriam's eyes. "I've enjoyed the time I've spent among people and as a part of a community. And, while it is true, Salem's people are far from perfect, what they are is worth protecting, and the best way I can protect them is by leaving."

"I don't understand. What makes you think you are a danger to us?"

Tobias stares at the faint outline of the Forbidden Mountains. "If I told you the truth about how I discovered the plague's cure, or why I call you Jenny, or where I found the wood for the flute...."

"Or why you call fire magic bloom?"

Tobias laughs, "Did I? But yes, that too. If I told you the answer to these questions, the best I could hope is you'd think me crazy and not believe a word I said. But what would be worse, much worse, is if you believe me. Then you, like me, would be guilty of heresy."

Staring at the wagon drawn by six horses that Tobias will take to the quarry, Miriam asks, "Do you think Micah will try to kill you?"

"Someone may try to kill me, but I'm not sure you can call that person Micah. I think Micah from before the plague is dead. In fact, I'm not sure that anyone survived the plague unchanged, and all need a new name to reflect the change. The plague may have affected Micah and Silas more than most because they've always had an inflated sense of self-importance stemming from God putting them into authority positions.

"But to answer your question, yes, I think someone will try. The morning after the caravan arrived back in Salem, Silas told me that Micah overpowered him and ran away too fast to catch. Silas lied, and he knows that I know he lied. Micah had a badly sprained ankle and could barely hobble."

"Silas helping Micah...That can't be right, can it? Still, I can't imagine life without you. You've changed. You're not the heartbroken, confused, frightened man who left Salem. Wherever you've been, whatever you've done has made you stronger, wiser, and something else. Since your return, you have touched the heart of every man, woman, and child. If only I could enter your mind and hear your thoughts and you could hear mine, perhaps I could convince you to stay."

# CHAPTER SEVEN

Tobias arrives at the quarry an hour before sunset and immediately sets about feeding and watering the horses.

When he finishes, he climbs onto a white sandstone ledge and sits beside several polished slate chisels and wooden mallets. *Nothing's changed. It's just like I left it nearly a year and a half ago, except the wooden lean-to has been torn apart, probably by Micah and company looking for me after I fled Salem. How stupid did they think I was? If I had come here, I'd have seen them coming miles off, and knowing every nook and cranny in these cliffs, they'd have never found me.*

Tobias hefts a chisel with his left hand and a mallet with his right. *It's like we've never been apart, but at the same time, I don't feel right about being here. When I promised a memorial for the plague victims, I thought I'd have to stay a year or maybe more, but now that Miriam tells me I don't, the sooner I leave the better.*

The night is overcast, with a cooling breeze carrying the chorus of frogs, cicadas, and the sporadic sounds of geese and ducks punctuated by the occasional owl blowing off the Blue River less than a quarter-mile distant. Tobias leaves the ledge and ambles to the fire pit, which was the first thing he built more than eight years ago. Using wood from a nearby stack, Tobias builds a small fire, then sets upright a three-legged backed stool which Asher, Miriam's mate, made for him.

A falling rock and wisp of a shadow moving across a sandstone ledge draws Tobias out of his reverie, but quickly resolves into a raccoon.

Tobias laughs, then quickly grows quiet. *Coming here might be a mistake. As much as I want to draw Micah into the open, I forgot how vulnerable I'd be. Not only is it hard to look out of the fire and see something moving among shadows, but it works just the opposite for someone peering out of the darkness. If Micah is intent on killing me, he's likely to succeed.*

That night, Tobias makes his bed beneath the wagon, where he feels confident he can safely sleep.

After breakfast, Tobias takes a mental inventory of the different varieties of stone and the difficulty of working each type. He then works up a series of preliminary sketches of different designs and calculates the quantity of stone required for each and the amount of time it would take to quarry.

*That first night, when I stood upon The Whitened Stone, I made two promises: Micah would pay with his life, and his victims would never be forgotten. Maybe what's needed is not one, but two memorials, so the victims of Micah's madness won't be lost among those who died of the plague.*

Hitching only two of the six horses, Tobias moves the wagon as close as possible to the seam of blue-gray slate. The slate is the easiest of all his choices to work, and its smooth surface will be the easiest to carve into or write upon the names of all who died.

By the fourth night, having quarried and loaded more than a sufficient quantity of the slate, Tobias,
growing restless to return to Salem, growls his frustration. *I can't leave, not if I'm going to give Micah every oppor-
tunity to kill me.*

The following day, jangled by waiting for an attack
that may never come, Tobias throws himself into quar-
rying the hardest stone to work, pink marble, to calm
his nerves. Where, how, or if he'll use it doesn't matter.
What's important is that it gives him somewhere to focus his attention, strength, and energy to the edge of
exhaustion.

That night, his muscles aching from overwork, Tobias sits in front of his campfire on the three-legged stool
and plays notes on Butterfly's flute that don't belong or
flow together. He names the dissonant conglomeration
*Waiting Is Hard.* Ten minutes into the tune, still struggling
to find a melody, he hears a rock dislodge, roll off a ledge,
and land with a thud perhaps a hundred feet away.

Tobias snaps to attention. After all the effort he's put
into minimizing the risk of ambush, how could he be
so stupid as to sit directly in front of the campfire? Hoping for another raccoon but fearing the worst, Tobias
reaches beneath the stool and grabs a sling loaded with a
heavy stone. Then, speaking loud enough for his voice
to echo and hide his fear, he says, "Hello, Micah. Why
don't you join me at the fire? I have leftover rabbit I
would gladly share."

"Hello, Tobias. I don't remember you being a musi-
cian, but after hearing you play, I'd say you're not."

Tobias searches the darkest shadows of the cliffs and ledges but sees nothing. "In my time away, I learned many things. How are you doing living off what you find? Or are you constantly starving? Please join me. I have more than I can eat."

"Me, hungry? No, I am fat and well-fed. I lack for nothing except your death, but soon I shall grow fat on that as well."

By following the sound of Micah's voice, Tobias distinguishes a shadow moving among shadows. He rolls off the stool in a single fluid motion and onto his side as an arrow embeds itself into the ground just behind the stool. Springing to his feet, Tobias zigzags behind the wagon, then laughs. "Still a lousy shot. You missed me when I crossed the Red River, and you missed me now."

"You and I both know that eventually I'll succeed, so please stop fighting. It'll save us both so much time and effort. Besides the bow, there are so many ways to kill you. You should have never left Salem. You should have never come back to Salem. And when you are dead, I shall again be High Priest."

"If Silas told you that, he lied. If you return to Salem, you'll be locked up. But not for long before you're executed for the mass murderer that you are. No one will ever accept you as High Priest. Silas will kill you when you are no longer useful."

Tobias hears branches snap, but not from where Micah's voice is coming. He moves in the sound's direction and swirls the sling, sending a missile ricocheting off a rock ledge.

A voice cries out.

Micah, stepping out of the shadow, shoots an arrow that is quickly followed by a shout of pain.

"Now that I've wounded you, you shall be easier to kill."

Keeping to the shadows, Tobias moves to a new position. "That's not me you wounded. It's somebody sent by Silas to kill you to make sure you never return to Salem."

Micah's silhouette stands in the open, near the edge of a rock ledge. "You know nothing. Why do you think Silas let me go the day he returned and found me in prison? Why do you think he has been helping…"

Tobias hears a sharp gasp followed by a dull thud as Micah falls twenty feet onto the quarry floor, an arrow sticking out of his back. Cautiously hurrying toward the sound of running footsteps, Tobias is in time to watch a silhouette disappear into the night.

When he returns, Micah is dead. Tobias drops to his knees, yanks the arrow out of Micah's back, then rolls him over. Micah's eyes are opened wide in shock. Tobias closes them and whispers. "As much as I hate what you've become, like me you were brought to this world aboard a cargo ship, brainwashed, and programmed to fulfill a specific function. Is it the fault of you or the programming that you became such a monster?"

Tobias looks towards—and in his mind, beyond— the Gateway Mountains, across the Great Emptiness, and the Flattop Mountains and into the Pathless Forest. *When I return to Salem, a man both bruised by a stone and shot by an arrow shall be easy to find. However, Silas and the assassin will have a day to invent their side of the story before I return, and having heard Micah's confession, Silas can't let me live.*

*But, compared to being covered in blood and waiting for the jaguars to come, Silas's threat is as nothing. What was it that saved me from the jaguars? Being innocent? Having truth on my side? No, what saved me then is what can save me now— entering the Circle of Always Becoming. But since leaving the Pathless Forest, it's something I can't do. My only hope is, as Butterfly said, that the purpose of the gods is to make sure what must happen happens and that what must happen is I'm to live.*

Tobias flings Micah's body over his shoulder and carries it down to the fire, to which he adds more wood. He changes clothes with Micah and props him up to look like he's sitting on the stool, providing his would-be assassin, should he return, a target for another try. After admiring his handiwork, Tobias hurries away and searches for Micah's camp, which, knowing the area around the quarry as well as he does, doesn't take long.

Along with a satchel filled with all manners of fruit, dried meat, cheese, raw carrots, and bread so fresh it's no more than a day old, Tobias finds a leather bag containing the original *Holy Book of Life* written by the hand of God. He spends the night at Micah's camp, and just before sunrise returns to find two arrows piercing the chest of the already dead Micah.

After removing Micah's weight in stone from the wagon, Tobias tosses Micah's body on top and starts back along the familiar road, which the horses will follow without someone to guide them.

When they get to the Leaving Tree, Tobias stops the wagon. From beneath the wagon seat, he retrieves the *Holy Book of Life* written by God's hand. Looking toward Salem, he thinks, *I'm not sure Silas will welcome the return of the original Holy Book, and until I am, it's safer here.*

Tobias quickly buries it beneath a heart-shaped stone. *Actually, it might be better if the people of Salem are forced to remember what is written within it and reawaken their memory of—and hopefully their love for—God. After all, what else do they have to give them hope, strength, and courage?*

Tobias slaps the rump of the lead horse and shouts, "Go on! Get going; you know the way!" As the wagon jolts forward, Tobias grabs his backpack, shakes his head, and laughs; *I've got to keep you close. What if somebody found you, looks inside, and finds my journals?*

By hurrying at a fast jog and cutting corners, Tobias arrives at Miriam's house several minutes before the wagon enters Salem. But as soon as he opens the door and sloughs off his backpack, he's rushed by four men armed with spears waiting just inside the door. Using a cane, Daniel Tallgrass, his left leg bandaged just below the groin, and Silas emerge from Tobias's bedroom, each holding one of Miriam's arms. Miriam wrenches herself from their grasp, rushes into Tobias' arms, then explodes into tears. "You shouldn't have come back! There's nothing I could do. There was no way to warn you."

Forcing a smile, Tobias holds Miriam at arm's length. "I knew Silas would be waiting. And if Micah were a better shot, we'd be burying Daniel and listening to Micah…"

Silas shouts, "So you admit it! Tobias Whitefield, I

am arresting you for the murder of Micah Skylark and the attempted murder of Daniel Tallgrass."

As Miriam is pulled off Tobias, he mouths, "Don't doubt me."

Silas and Daniel lead the procession, with an armed man on either side of Tobias and two behind. Tobias winks and nods as he passes Joshua Nightwind holding two young girls' hands while a boy rides upon his shoulders, pulling at his hair.

The procession ends at the very cell in which he had locked Micah.

When the outer door is closed, it's as dark as the Healing Place. Sitting calmly in the center of the cell, Tobias embraces the darkness the way he did with Butterfly in the healing place.

• • •

Holding a single lit candle, Joshua Nightwind peers through the narrow window of Tobias's cell. "I'm sorry it's so late. Silas didn't want any visitors until morning, but I insisted by asserting my rights as Acting High Priest."

"Acting High Priest? I'm surprised. Silas said he had someone else in mind."

"After I saw you arrested, I spread the word, and with a half-dozen others, I went to Silas and insisted that your trial had to be open and fair. I think Silas got rattled, and long story short he had no choice but to offer me, the only *priest* he's got around to making, the job. I'm sorry, but I'm not allowed to open the door. Silas is afraid that you could overpower the guards and me, so we have to talk through the door."

"I'm, of course, pleased to see you, but I am surprised Miriam isn't with you."

"Silas has placed her under house arrest."

"Miriam terrifies Silas. After all, she is far more respected and admired than he. So what evidence, and I use the term loosely, does Silas have?"

"He has a sworn statement from Daniel Tallgrass made under penalty of death if proven false. Daniel claims that at Silas's behest, he had been tracking Micah for some time and had followed him to the quarry where he saw Micah about to kill you. He claims he disturbed Micah's aim just enough that Micah's shot went wide. Daniel claims he bruised his shoulder against a stone when he wrestled Micah into submission. Then, as he was marching Micah into your camp to prove Micah was no longer a danger to you, he claims you went crazy and killed Micah with two arrows to the chest. He claims you would have killed him if he hadn't run away. As it was, you only wounded him in the thigh."

"That's quite a story."

"But is it true?"

"Do you mean is it more believable to a prejudiced panel of judges than any story I can tell? Most certainly."

"That's not what I asked, but I see your point. Truth is whatever people choose to believe. Still, your only chance is to tell your side of the story."

"I'm not going to enter a plea or defend myself."

"What? Why?"

"I don't have any physical evidence I can present, which means it's my word against Daniel's, and Daniel's story is going to carry more weight because he has staked his life on the truth of what he's said, whereas people will think I'll lie to save mine. No, I've got to leave it up to God to sort things out."

Joshua shakes his head. "I admire your faith, but sometimes you've got to be practical. Sometimes God needs our help to make things come out right. If you do nothing, Silas, Daniel, and the rest will get away with the murder of Micah and yourself. And once they do, there will be no end to the evil they will bring down upon the people of Salem."

Tobias laughs. "For the High Priest, acting or not, that borders on heresy. Besides, there are you and Miriam to stop him. For a short time, while people struggle to come to terms with a new reality, Silas and Daniel and their lies might prevail, but that won't last. As soon as people awaken to remembering how it was before the plague, they will demand a return to the way it was. Then Silas and company will face a day of reckoning."

Joshua shakes his head. "I don't know, maybe. But if you defend yourself, the entire town would show up, and..."

"The town would split into factions, and suddenly you have neighbor hating neighbor, something as deadly as any plague. Salem has done without me for more than a year and can continue without me."

Joshua sighs loud and long. "It shouldn't have to.

196

Once you were a vital part of Salem and can be again. But if you've made up your mind and won't listen to reason, there's nothing for me to do."

In the morning, Tobias wakes remembering a dream. He saw the four rivers of the Great Valley, their color the color of their names, the Red, Blue, Yellow, and Green, come together, each from a different direction, and meet at a single point. The rivers pivoted about a central place, their colors swirling behind them in a beautiful spiral pattern, and out of the central point emerged a tower that twirled and turned to bark. The bark swirled, and a tree grew up and spread out in over-arching branches. The leaves were a swirl of red, green, yellow, and blue. Then, out of the southwest, came a crow that perched on the tree's pinnacle. But when the crow left, he had transformed into a white falcon that circled higher and higher until it disappeared into a green sun.

*If instead of a White Falcon, Corvus had become the Sun-fisher, I would know my life was over, but now I know I will live, no longer as Corvus but as White Falcon.*

At precisely one o'clock, Tobias, accompanied by Joshua Nightwind, is led upstairs to the Elder's meeting room, which can seat a hundred people and provides standing room for half that many again. As he enters through a side room, Tobias smiles. As he hoped, the room is empty except for a dozen people seated in the front row and four people sitting in the back row.

Tobias, standing in front of the defendant's chair, watches six men solemnly parade in from either side and stand behind their chairs. Silas, wearing a robe made of a reddish-brown shiny fur, a necklace made of the seashells, and holding an ivory scepter, makes a grand entry.

Silas spreads his arms wide, "Be seated."

After a long, slow look across the empty seats, Silas says, "The case of Tobias Whitefield, charged with the murder of Micah Skylark and the attempted murder of Daniel Tallgrass is now underway. Tobias Whitefield, how do you plead?"I

Joshua Nightwind rises. "Against his counsel's advice, Tobias Whitefield refuses to enter a plea. Instead, he leaves the verdict and his fate in God's hand."

Silas moves his mouth around like he is chewing. "The court takes note and accepts Tobias Whitefield's refusal to enter a plea, which, according to law, the court understands as an admission of guilt. Tobias Whitefield, do you have anything to say which we might consider in rendering a decision as to your punishment?"

Smiling like he has eaten too much of a delicious meal and has now grown sleepy, Tobias mumbles, "What? Oh, no. Except, not that it matters, but yes, I ask that you remember Micah killed thirty-eight, and I saved three hundred eighty-four."

Silas grins his toothy grin at Tobias, "You're right, it doesn't matter. The court will reconvene in one hour."

Tobias, accompanied by Joshua, is escorted back to his cell. Joshua slides a torch into a wall socket just outside the cell door before allowing himself to be locked in with Tobias, who whistles a song that ends on a rising crescendo.

"How can you be so calm? You and I both know the question in Silas's mind isn't if you're going to die but how."

*Because of my White Falcon dream, I have faith I shall live. What is Joshua's source of faith? Or is Joshua's faith clinging not onto a cliff made of granite, but a cliff made of hope and wishful thinking? What would it take for him to let go and get swept away in a torrent of despair? What will it take him to become the leader Salem desperately needs?*

"Perhaps my death will be the wake-up call people need. Silas's power doesn't come from God; it comes from people not willing to stand up to him. To defeat Silas and his ilk, people need to rekindle their love and relationship with God and be willing to stand up to Silas. You have what it takes to lead the people back to God, and Miriam has proven she has what it takes to stand up to Silas."

Joshua shakes his head, and as it drops to his chest, he says, "I don't know, maybe." After closing his eyes, Joshua swallows, then begins moving his mouth in silent conversation with God.

Tobias watches Butterfly, transformed into her namesake, flit through the Pathless Forest.

• • •

Precisely an hour later, Tobias and Joshua are back in their seats, staring up at Silas and the rest of the Council of Elders. The people who earlier were in the front row are still there, but those sitting in the back are gone.

Looking down upon Tobias, Silas tries to hide his excitement with a somber frown. "Tobias Whitefield, you have been found not just guilty but profoundly guilty of all charges, and it's hereby decreed that your name, as well as the names of your wife, Rebecca, and daughter, Naomi, shall be stricken from the *Holy Book of Life*, thus condemning you and your family to wander in outer darkness, never to return into the presence of God."

*Is it possible,* Tobias wonders, *for Rebecca and Naomi, who according to the Holy Book of Life are already in God's presence, to be forced out of His presence by a verdict rendered by people and their names deleted from a book I had hidden away?*

"It is the further decision of the court that lifetime exile is not sufficient punishment. Living in exile would be a death sentence for anyone else, but for you, it is no punishment. Therefore, this court decrees that tonight, at sunset, you shall be taken to Temple Hill, where a pole shall be set. You shall be tied to said pole and burned until you are dead."

Joshua stands and shouts, "No! Nowhere in the *Holy Book of Life* does it say being burned alive is an acceptable punishment."

"Really? Do you have the original copy that I might check? No? Well then, we're going to have to go with what I remember. After all, I am God's chosen to be Chief Elder and have committed to memory every word. In fact, the section dealing with the duties, responsibilities, and laws of both the Priests and the Elders is in the process of being rewritten from the combined memories of all who were present on the Final Day of Creation, just as Tobias suggested."

"If Tobias must die, then do it humanely!"

"Normally I'd agree, but since Tobias was found not just guilty but profoundly guilty of the charge of murder, then a more extreme execution is not only warranted but demanded under the law. Take away the prisoner. He is to see no one until time for the execution, although he is allowed a final meal."

Tobias touches his heart, the center of his forehead then clasps his hands and bows slightly from the waist. "Thank you, but I prefer to die with an empty stomach."

Silas slams his palms down on the desktop as he rises and says, "If I could have thought of a worse punishment, you wouldn't be getting off so lightly."

Tobias, remembering Butterfly's description of the punishment for killing a jaguar, breaks into laughter as Silas stomps out of the room, leading a confused-looking procession.

Joshua, along with four guards, escorts Tobias back to his cell. "I can't say I'm surprised at the verdict. But the punishment? If I get enough people together, I'm sure I can stop it."

Tobias places a hand on Joshua's shoulder. "No. Joshua, promise me you won't do anything stupid. I know that for you to let things happen the way they must will require both tremendous courage and unwavering faith in God, but you must find the strength to do both. Otherwise, I fear anger shall poison your spirit and you will become all that you hate in Silas. Remember when you said you knew nothing of becoming a priest and I said that more important than knowing the rites and rituals was compassion? Quench your anger with compassion and become the man Salem needs."

After a half-dozen stuttered attempts at coherent speech, Joshua mumbles, "I still think God can use a hand about now."

When they reach the long hallway leading to the prison cell, two guards push themselves between Joshua and Tobias.

Joshua shouts, "What's going on? I'm the High Priest. I have the right to be with him."

"Orders from the Chief Elder."

Tobias whispers, "Joshua, remember; don't do anything stupid."

As soon as he enters the cell, Tobias sits with his legs crossed and back straight. *How is it that hearing Silas pronounce my sentence has allowed my anger to drain away?*

• • •

Joshua opens the cell door. "Tobias, it's time."

When Tobias doesn't respond, Joshua rushes over and checks Tobias's neck for a heartbeat, then kneeling in front of him, shakes his shoulders and says, "Tobias, it's Joshua. It's time."

Tobias sighs and slowly stretches. "What day is it?"

"What day? It's Thursday, August 30th."

"August 30th? Late summer? Good, I shall be at my home by Floating Fire Lake in time for harvest."

Joshua looks from Tobias to the two armed guards standing on either side of Tobias. "I think he's lost his mind."

As Joshua walks beside Tobias, he presses a small vial into Tobias's hand and whispers. "Miriam has prepared a potion. Take it just before they tie you to the post. You will be unconscious before the flames reach you."

Tobias withdraws his still-empty hand. "Tell Miriam...no, tell her nothing. I'll tell her when I see her."

"But you won't see her. She isn't allowed anywhere near where you are to be..."

The walk to the summit of Temple Hill takes less than fifteen minutes. It's a warm, clear, fragrant evening filled with birdsong. It reminds Tobias of how he was programmed to remember Creation's Final Day, when he, Rebecca, and all the Four Hundred were created. The only differences are that his life is ending instead of beginning, and the small black cloud growing in the west is moving quickly towards him.

Only the Chief Elder, the full complement of Elders, a dozen supporters who will soon swell the ranks of Priests, and Joshua Nightwind are in attendance.

Tobias smiles as he watches a crow land on top of the pole and squawks out a medley of different sounds. "Old Friend, it's good you are here to bear witness. Tell whoever will listen to a crow that I remembered how to enter the Circle."

Daniel Tallgrass grins as he ties Tobias's hands behind the pole. He hisses, "In a few minutes, the flames will bite into your flesh, melting it, every nerve and muscle screaming with pain, and you can do nothing."

Silas solemnly reads the charges, the verdict, and the punishment ordained, then asks Tobias for any final words.

"My body may die, but I shall live in every blade of grass, and tree, and..."

Silas barks, "That's it? No begging for mercy? No protestation of your innocence?"

Tobias responds by whistling *The Flight of the White Falcon*.

Silas snarls, "How does it feel to know that soon you shall join your mate and barely a daughter in outer darkness, where all shall die from loneliness for want of God's forgiveness?"

Tobias laughs. "You may kill me, but God, who sees all, knows who the true murderers are and will not allow you and Daniel to go unpunished."

Silas scrambles up the woodpile, slaps Tobias hard enough to make his lip bleed, then yells, "Joshua, as acting High Priest, do your duty. Light the fire!"

Joshua drops the torch. "No."

Silas whirls and looks into the shocked faces of the gathered men. He picks up the torch and proclaims in a loud voice, "Daniel Tallgrass, by my authority of Chief Elder, I hereby proclaim that in accordance with the laws laid out within the *Holy Book of Life*, you are High Priest."

Joshua yells, "There's no such law, and you know it!"

"Do I? We'll have to see what's recorded in the *Holy*

*Book of Life* after Daniel and the rest of the Order of Priests finish composing it. As your first official act as High Priest, Daniel, light the fire."

Joshua turns to walk away.

Tobias shouts, "Joshua, don't doubt me now!"

Joshua stops and turns to face Tobias.

Daniel picks up the torch and grins at Tobias as the sky explodes with lightning and thunder sharing the same heartbeat, killing Silas instantly and flattening Daniel to the ground.

Daniel scrambles to his feet and stands dazed, repeatedly shouting, "Silas made me."

The remaining Elders look at each other. No one stops Daniel as he takes off running. And no one stops Joshua as he climbs the stack of wood and unties Tobias.

• • •

The thunder crack, announcing Silas's death and knocking Daniel senseless, wakes Salem out of its stupor. Within moments, the streets fill with people looking for the thunder's source and to their amazement see only a single, small black cloud.

Joshua leads Tobias down Temple Hill to Town Square Park, where everyone is gathering, then steps onto the wooden platform where ten days earlier he stood and conducted the Ceremony of Remembrance and Release. He raises both hands for silence.

"People of Salem, Silas Windcatcher is dead, killed by an act of God. Before Daniel Tallgrass ran off, he proclaimed that he bore false testimony against Tobias at the Chief Elder's urging.

"My friends, the people of Salem, have been sorely tested. Within six weeks, we experienced certain death by plague, the miraculous cure provided by Tobias Whitefield, the mass murder committed by Micah Skylark, and the distortion of God's laws by Silas Windcatcher.

"There are some who will say this calamity is more than can be endured. After all, we are few, and without the *Holy Book of Life* to guide us, how shall we live? We shall live because we are a living, vital people. Those of the Four Hundred who still live, who were present upon the Final Day of Creation, have forever engraved upon their hearts those words, those first words which God spoke out of the Flame of Ever-Changing Color that gave off no heat, 'Behold! I am your God, and you are My people. Fear not! For I am a God of love!'

"And I, along with the collective memory of everyone alive that day, shall reconstruct the *Holy Book of Life* without error, so that the words of God shall once again speak to all the generations to come.

"Of the Order of Priests that God chose upon the Final Day of Creation, none remain. Although Silas filled out the Council of Elders ranks by appointing men to the positions, I do not believe these appointments are valid. Each Elder's individual role in recent events will need to be determined that all may be held accountable.

"How we shall choose who to fulfill these roles, I don't know. At the recommendation of Tobias Whitefield, Silas Windcatcher chose me as acting High Priest, but this in no way should influence any decision. If I were to make any recommendations, I should nominate Tobias Whitefield for the position of Chief Elder."

The crowd murmurs amongst itself as Tobias climbs to stand beside Joshua. Tobias smiles as he sees Miriam push her way through the crowd to stand in the front row, with Andrew, Anna, and Abigail at her side.

Tobias does as Joshua did and raises his hands to quiet the crowd. "Joshua, thank you for those kind words, but I implore you, do not let it be so. Instead, I suggest that Joshua Nightwind continue in the role of High Priest and ask that you consider for the role of Chief Elder someone who has earned your love and respect through her hard work and compassion: Miriam Sweetwater."

An electrical undercurrent of approval sweeps through the crowd as Tobias extends his hand to Miriam and helps her and her young charges onto the stand.

Miriam says, "Friends, this is entirely unexpected. I don't know how to react, and I doubt you do either. Let's not rush into decisions. We have time. Between the food salvaged from the burned warehouses, what the Elders harvested and stored in the Community Center, and the crops remaining to be harvested, we will not only survive this winter, but we shall..." Miriam turns and looks toward Joshua, "...with God's help, prosper. Let us now return to our homes and give thanks to God for all He has done for us this day. In an hour, let us reassemble here and celebrate. Let us make this day, like the Anniversary of the Final Day of Creation, a day of remembrance and celebration."

Miriam whispers something to Joshua, who takes charge of the children standing beside her, then she and Tobias return to her house.

On the kitchen table is Tobias's journal, laid open. Miriam hands it to him. "I never understood why you never went anywhere without your backpack. Now I know, and because I do, I want you to leave Salem immediately and never return. I started reading from when you, calling yourself Corvus, sat atop the mountains you call the Way Forward Mountains located beyond the Forbidden Mountains, which you call something else. And I read about the creature you called Butterfly and stopped reading when you and she acted in unnatural ways."

Tobias says nothing, but takes the journal and replaces it in his backpack.

"Now I know the answers to all the questions I wanted you to answer, except one: Why you called me Jenny."

Tobias shrugs but says nothing.

"So, what's the real reason you returned when you did? Did something happen to Butterfly? Is she dead?"

"Yes, Butterfly is dead. Butterfly taught me the importance of living in a community, but knowing what I know and having seen what I've seen, I was afraid to return to Salem. But if you had read on, you would have learned how I returned to the Ethereal Glade, and when I spoke to the Goddess she unstopped my eyes, and I saw a glowing orange snake, which I now know were the torches used to light the caravan's night journey. She unstopped my ears, and I heard the wails of people mourning the dead. Then she told me I must return; my people needed me."

"If Joshua finds out you crossed the Forbidden Mountains, he'll be forced to send you into lifetime exile. He won't want to, but he'll have no choice unless you leave before he gets here. And I hate to think what he would do if he learned you no longer believe in God, but believe in a Goddess that lives in a swamp, and something called the Circle of Always Becoming, and what you and that creature did…"

"Butterfly was not a creature. She did not look like us, but she was a woman made beautiful by the compassion, love, and empathy she felt for all that lives.

"When she found me near death, I was a stranger, so unlike anyone she had ever known, and yet it never occurred to her to walk away and let me die. She saw that despite appearances, we are far more similar than different. If the situation was reversed, would you have acted so nobly? If not, why? Why should someone you call a creature act more nobly than one of God's children?

"But more than that, she taught me to see how all life everywhere is interconnected. She showed me how God surrounds and envelops all that lives, and is not Someone who has left and we'll only meet again after death. Until the people of Salem stop seeing themselves and the domesticated plants and animals as superior to the rest of nature, Salem's people will always be strangers in a strange land and never find a home on Eden."

Tobias pauses and feels Miriam's anger rise. "Now

that you know other people live on Eden, what will you do with that knowledge?"

"I'm going to forget what nobody needs to know."

Tobias tosses on his backpack and turns to go. "Wait, if you started reading when I arrived at the lake, you know about Erik and Erik's grandfather, Miles."

"I read it, but it made no sense to me."

"*Tambour, leave my flute.*"

Tobias opens his backpack and takes out Butterfly's flute. "Butterfly wants you to have her flute."

Miriam recoils. "I don't want anything that belonged to that creature."

"When you thought I made it, the flute was beautiful, but now you know Butterfly made it, it becomes ugly? What does that say about you? Take it; it's made from the wood of a wisdom tree."

"Wisdom tree?"

"Butterfly believes that wisdom is never lost but can be found in all things everywhere, even in trees."

Miriam shakes her head and backs away from it.

Tobias replaces the flute into the backpack, then turning to face Miriam, touches his heart, the center of his forehead, and clasps his hands, and as he does, he says, "With an open heart, an open mind, and full intent, I bid you goodbye. May God always bless and keep you."

Tobias, leaving, meets Joshua arriving with the three children in tow. The children walk past Tobias and into the house.

Tobias grasps Joshua's left shoulder, "You and Miriam are the future of Salem. Don't ask what's next, but let tomorrow fall like spring rain upon a world forever becoming alive. Always stay within the moment, never looking farther into the future than a single heartbeat."

"The way you talk, it sounds like if you're leaving."

Tobias nods.

"But there's no reason to."

"When I first met Miriam at the caravan, I promised her that I'd stay only until Salem's survival is secure, and from what Miriam reported tonight, that has happened. Besides, Eden is a big place, and the people of Salem have their hands full rebuilding their future, which leaves only me to explore it and learn its secrets. But as I leave, I ask that you accept this flute as a gift. Perhaps, one day, if Salem is ever again in peril, someone shall learn to play its secrets, and I shall hear and return."

Joshua takes the flute. "It's beautiful; it's heavier than I expected. It feels tingly, almost like it's alive. Thank you, I shall treasure the flute as a symbol of our undying friendship." He then grabs Tobias's arm above the elbow. "My friend, travel safe. And remember, wherever you go, Salem will always be your home."

• • •

Ten days after leaving Miriam's house and Tobias behind, White Falcon stands atop the Red Tower. An hour ago, as he lay in the Doorway's warm, soothing waters, he dreamt he was standing atop the Red Tower. Gathered about him were Erik and Jenny, Tobias and Rebecca, Corvus and the Goddess of the Glade, Tambour and Butterfly. He then walked to the edge of the Red Tower and kept walking.

White Falcon looks toward the Yellow Eye of the Great Bull that has just emerged in the deepening twilight and sighs contentedly. "In my life, I've lived many lives. I lived as Erik, an angry young man who was willing to risk a forty percent mortality rate as a first-generation colonist to get off-world. I lived as Tobias, a man of deep faith and a strong sense of duty. I lived as Corvus, a man who never felt at home or comfortable with where he was or what he knows. I lived as Tambour, a man who, through the love of a blind empath, found a connection with all life everywhere.

"Now I am asked to leave behind all those lives and become White Falcon. But who is White Falcon that he can walk off the Red Tower's edge and not fall? Has he become immaterial? Or do the laws of nature no longer apply?"

White Falcon laughs as he spreads his arms and slowly pivots in place, speaking in a deep, resonating voice. "No, my friends. I exist in a world of rocks, trees, wind, and rain. A world of incredible beauty and hidden dangers that one day I'll leave as my body dies. But I also live in a timeless world, where trees contain wisdom, crows talk and transform into men, and butterflies become goddesses. A world where I can speak to jaguars and enter a Circle of Always Becoming, never knowing where I end and where all that is begins.

"To walk off the Red Tower's edge doesn't demand courage, only the belief that what can't be seen is just as real as what can be."

White Falcon then drops to his knees and from his backpack removes two polished slate chisels he took from Tobias' workshop in Salem. He begins carving a vault in which he'll place the *Holy Book of Life* written by the hand of God, and one day, his completed journal—leaving it to the gods, if and when they are ever discovered.

## ABOUT THE AUTHOR

James Argos is a third generation Colorado native. His passion lies at the intersection of archaeology, mythology, Jungian psychology, and cosmology. He enjoys painting, writing poetry, working with the I Ching, and solitary desert retreats.